Million Dollar Mates

Other series by Cathy Hopkins
Mates, Dates
Truth, Dare, Kiss or Promise
Cinnamon Girl
Zodiac Girls

And, coming soon
Million Dollar Mates: Paparazzi Princess

Cathy Hopkins

Million Dollar Mates

SIMON & SCHUSTER

First published in Great Britain in 2010 by Simon and Schuster UK Ltd
A CBS COMPANY

This edition published as a covermount exclusive for *Shout* magazine in 2011

Simon & Schuster UK Ltd
1st Floor
222 Gray's Inn Road
London WC1X 8HB

A CIP catalogue record for this book
is available from the British Library.

ISBN 978-0-85707-482-9

1 3 5 7 9 10 8 6 4 2

Typeset by M Rules
Printed by CPI Cox & Wyman, Reading, Berkshire RG1 8EX

www.simonandschuster.co.uk
www.cathyhopkins.com

For Greta Brenman,
who truly was a Million Dollar Mate.

1

Shopping for Boys

'Reasons I'd like to stay living at Gran's,' I said as Pia and I left the heat of the August sunshine behind us and stepped through automatic doors into the air-conditioned Village area of Westfield shopping mall. 'One: I can walk to school from there—'

'You mean *run*. You're always late,' Pia interrupted as we headed for the escalator and took in the wealth of shops stretching before us.

'OK, run. Good point. Imagine if I lived further away.'

'Nightmare,' said Pia. 'You'd never make it.'

'Exactly. Numero two: Gran's house is in the next street to yours.'

Pia linked her arm through mine. 'And we need to be near each other, especially after everything you've been through in the last year. End of story. You ought to be allowed to stay on compassionate grounds.'

'True. It would be cruel and heartless to separate us.'

We stepped onto the escalator and floated up under the vast pink roof from which an enormous chandelier was suspended. It looked like an explosion of raindrops, sparkling in space. The Village area of the mall is our favourite part. We call it Poshville because it's where the seriously upmarket shops like Dior, Tiffany, Gucci and Prada are located. We like to window-shop and dream, then hang out in one of the seating areas in the middle, where someone has kindly arranged armchairs and a coffee table on a carpet next to a massive flower arrangement that looks like it cost a bomb. As we got off the escalator, I noticed today's display was a chaotic mix of pink orchids with twigs, about four foot tall.

Pia pulled me over to look at a window display of awesome shoes with killer heels. 'Anyway, I need you round the corner so we can still go to school together when term starts again. I need you close to borrow your make-up, to watch telly together, to have sleepovers. No. You moving is so *not* an option. Third reason?'

'Gran's is two streets away from Tom Robertson's house, he who is the love of my life, and the keeper of my heart.'

'Of course . . . The keeper of your heart?'

'Yes. He keeps it in a small jar on his desk.'

Pia pulled a face. 'Haha. Yuck. I meant, how can he be keeper of your heart when you haven't even talked to him?'

'Because he is The One and the fact we haven't talked yet is a minor detail. Most of the school hasn't met him properly yet, seeing as he only arrived at the end of last term. All the more reason for me to stay living nearby so that I can accidentally on purpose bump into him. Josh Tyler told our Charlie that Tom's last girlfriend was a brunette, so I reckon I'm in with a chance.'

There's a sad shortage of boy talent at our school, so when Tom arrived looking tall and lean, with moody good looks and tousled brown hair, he caused quite a stir.

'You would be anyway: you're the best-looking girl in our year by a long way,' said Pia, my totally unbiased best mate.

'I am so *not* gorgeous: my shoulders are too broad, my legs are too skinny, my boobs are growing way too fast and my hair is a nightmare unless I use hair straighteners, plus my mouth is too wide. On bad days I look like a duck – a duck with big boobs.' I know I can look OK if I make an effort but best-looking girl in our year? Definitely not.

'You don't look like a duck, idiot. And your chestie bits are fine. Boys *like* girls with curves. Any other reasons for not wanting to move?'

Pia is curvy herself, though she's smaller than me, but is totally cool with her shape and always dresses to show it off, whereas I try and hide mine in my indie clothes and layers, much to her annoyance.

'OK, well, Dave likes it at Gran's.' (Dave is my cat.)

'Best reason of all. Cats don't like to move and he's been moved already once this year.'

'I know. Too much disruption. It took him weeks to settle in. Me too. Everyone should give us a break. Both of us.'

'When do you think you'll find out?' asked Pia.

'This week, maybe even today. Dad said he'd ring if it was good news, not that it'll be good to me.'

'No, it'll be totally tragic news. I hope he doesn't get it,' said Pia.

My dad had applied for a job as manager of some boring old apartment complex in town. If he got it, it came with a house attached – which meant my brother Charlie and me moving from Gran's house, where we'd lived since Mum died nine months ago, and in with Dad, who we hadn't lived with since my parents split up six years ago. We'd lived with Mum after their divorce, though had always seen Dad pretty regularly.

Mum's death changed everything – we not only lost her, we lost our home too. We couldn't stay where we were without an adult and although staying with my aunt Maddie was suggested, she lives with her boyfriend in a one-bed flat and didn't really want us there cramping her style (or lack of it lately). Nor did she want to have to move into our old house to look after us, even though Mum was her older sister. Luckily, Gran came forward like a shot with the offer to stay with her, because Dad wasn't in any position to have us descend on him either. He managed a très posho hotel in Mayfair and lived in. He's never needed a normal house with a kitchen because everything is always laid on wherever he's worked. And there was definitely no room for two tall teenagers at that hotel. Charlie's five foot eleven and I'm five nine, so there was no tucking us away in a linen cupboard.

Anyway, I like it at Gran's. I feel settled there. OK, so it isn't totally ideal. Charlie has to sleep on a pull-out sofa in the living room, and my bed is in the room that Gran used to use as her painting studio, but we get by. Dave likes it there too. Gran lives on a quiet tree-lined street, so not much traffic for him to dodge.

Since Mum died, Dad had been looking at all sorts of options so that Charlie and I could live with him permanently. He'd even explored the idea of moving out to the countryside so we could be together, but then this job came up. General Manager of an apartment block in Knightsbridge, which comes with a three-bedroom house. 'Might be perfect,' said Dad. *Might not be*, I thought. It feels like too much has been happening too fast lately. Too much change. Like my world's been turned upside-down. Some days I don't know what's hit me. One day I was happy. Mum was alive. I had my own room. I felt safe. Normal. No worries. Next day, I found out that she had cancer and I couldn't take anything for granted any more.

Being at Gran's has allowed me to catch my breath a little, plus Gran gets how I feel. Granddad died a few years back and now her eldest daughter had gone too, so she knows just how it feels to lose the people you love. Sometimes a song will come on the radio and her eyes mist over or someone will say something to me that reminds me of Mum and I'll choke up. Gran and I just give each other a hug at times like that. We know that there's nothing we can say to bring them back. We hug a lot. So, no, I really don't want Dad to get this new job on top of everything else. I want to stay put.

Pia and I cruised down the line of shops, like we did most days in the summer holidays, stopping occasionally to look in a window. We'd been saving for ages for this particular trip and we both had twenty-five quid in our pockets and permission to spend. Bliss. I wanted to get a top to wear for an event we'd been notified was going to happen soon after we got back to school. It's to raise funds to build a new library. A bunch of us had been invited along as representatives: a few mega brains from science and languages, prefects, a few of us from sports. I'm our school's best swimmer which is why I got invited. Pia is ace at drama and singing so she's in, and word has it that as Tom is a top football player – he's already on the school team – he'll probably be there too.

'This money-raising thing might be my best chance to meet Tom,' I said, as I peered at the price of a pair of silver sneakers. 'OK, me and every other girl there . . . which is why I have to dress to get him to notice me. That first impression is the one that lasts. It'll be the perfect place. I'll ask someone on our team to do the honours and introduce us. I can see it all in my head. I will be wearing something fabulous, looking graceful, elegant and sophisticated. Someone will say, "Oh, Tom, have you met Jess? She's our best hope for junior swimming champion, don't you know?" I'll smile modestly. He'll look into my eyes. I'll look into his. There'll be a moment of magic and he will be mine. I can't wait. I'll say something witty, then leave.'

'I think you should ignore him, act like you haven't even noticed him,' said Pia. 'I read somewhere that in the art of flirting, a girl must always leave them wanting more.'

'Maybe. He is pretty cool, isn't he?'

'So outcool him. Boys like him have girls falling at their feet all the time, so you need to seem unavailable, glacial even. Be, like, whatever, I am so not interested.

Boys like him like the chase, a challenge; what they can't have, not what they can.'

'You're so right, P. Anyway, he might fancy *you*,' I said. He might, too. Boys always seem to like Pia. Not just because she's pretty – which she is in a tomboy, cheeky cherub kind of way, with short, layered dark hair, big hazel eyes, great cheekbones and a wide mouth which is always smiling – no, boys like her because she is FUN.

'Nah. He looks arrogant, like he's so good-looking and he knows he could have anyone as his girlfriend.'

'Which is why I want to make him remember *me*,' I said. 'We're about the same height, which is good. I know because I stood behind him in the lunch queue just before we broke up for summer. He was holding an egg-and-cress sandwich.'

'Ah. Is that why you switched from your usual cheese-and-tomato?'

'Yes. It'll be our thing,' I said. 'If he sees me eating it, he'll think we have something in common.'

Pia pulled a face. 'Egg and cress? Egg and *cress*? Like, how uncool is that?'

I nodded. 'No, others may have hearts and roses, we will have egg and cress. Don't ever let it be said that I don't know what's what when it comes to romance.'

Pia cracked up. It's one of the things I like about her. She laughs at my rubbish jokes. 'I despair,' she said.

*

After half an hour of looking around, I spotted a silver top in a boutique window that looked the biz. The shop was on the edge of Poshville and there were posters all over the window announcing that everything was fifty per cent off in the summer sale. Everything MUST go. Knock down prices. *Excellent.*

We were about to walk in when I saw a girl about my age with her mum. They were chatting away, arms linked. I immediately got a lump in my throat. Shopping with Mum was one of the things I missed most. It was our girl-time together, a bit of window-shopping, then she'd always buy me something, even when we were broke – like a pretty hair clip from Claire's or Accessorize, or a lippie from The Body Shop, then it was hot chocolates at the nearest café, then home. She was great to shop with. She knew all there was to know about fashion because, before she got too ill, she worked as a personal shopper for Selfridges and, before that, for an online website which specialised in trend forecasting in fashion. She went to all the shows during Fashion Week and we always had all the most current glossy magazines at home: *Vogue*, *In-Style*, *Harper's Bazaar*, *Marie Claire*, *Grazia*. I loved going through the pages showing the latest designer collections with her, as she used to let me help her pick out what to get for her clients.

Sometimes it hurt so much that she'd gone, I didn't

know what to do with myself. I couldn't handle the pain, it was like a bottomless hole that had opened up inside me and was going to pull me into it. And there was nothing I could take for it, no ointment to rub in, no tablet to swallow. Charlie, on one of the few occasions that he'd spoken to me about Mum's death, said that he always tries to think of something else to get through times like that. He makes himself do some kind of activity to take his mind off what he's feeling, like he'll accelerate into anything that will distract him. Lately I've been trying to do that too.

Don't dwell, move on, I told myself as I took a deep breath and pulled Pia into the shop.

A stick-thin assistant glanced up, did a quick flick up and down taking in our jeans and Converse sneakers (mine coral, Pia's grey patchwork), then raised an eyebrow, as if to say, *Are you sure you should be in here?*

I wasn't going to let her intimidate me. Whenever I went shopping with Mum, she'd say, 'Always remember, *we're* the customers.'

I pointed at the mannequin wearing my top in the window. 'How much is that top?' I asked. 'Is it in the sale?'

'The silver one?'

I nodded.

'You're in luck. It is,' she said, with the hint of a smile.

Fifty per cent off, I thought. *Great. Can't cost much, then.* And Tom will be *bound* to notice me if I'm wearing it. It'll look perfect with my black jeans. All the mags say silver is a good colour for girls with chestnut brown hair and blue eyes like mine. Cornflower blue, Mum always used to say. *Tom, baby, prepare to be smitten*, I thought.

The assistant fetched the top from the window. There was no price tag. 'Does madam want to try it on?'

I nodded. Another magazine tip. You can never tell the cut of anything until you've got it on. I followed Miss Prissy Knickers assistant to the changing room and Pia came in with me. There was a blonde girl about our age going into the one next door to ours. She was loaded down with outfits to try on. I drew the curtain of our changing room and pulled on the silver top.

'Looks fabulous,' declared Pia. 'Hair loose down your back, bit of lippie and Tom bites the dust.'

We high fived each other, then I got changed and took the top to the till.

'That'll be two hundred and fifty pounds,' said the assistant.

'I . . . wha . . .' I spluttered.

'Two hundred and fifty pounds,' she repeated, looking bored.

'I thought you said it was in the sale.'

'It is. It *was* five hundred.'

I could see that the assistant was enjoying my discomfort. *OK*, I thought. *Two can play at this game.* 'What do you think, Pia?' I said. 'Only two hundred and fifty. It *is* lovely. Shall I get two?'

Pia got what I was up to straight away. 'Yes. Maybe. Do you have it in any other colours?' she asked the assistant.

The assistant opened and closed her mouth like a fish. 'I . . . yes . . . In the back. In black.'

'Great,' I said. 'I don't have enough cash on me for both but I'll go to the cash machine. See you in ten minutes.'

I made myself stand tall and walked out of the shop with Pia close behind.

'Jess Hall,' said Pia. 'That was a big fat fib.'

'No, it wasn't. I *didn't* have enough cash on me, that was the truth.'

Pia laughed. Behind her, I could see that the girl who had been trying things on in the next-door changing room had taken her items to the till, about five of them from what I could see, and the assistant had begun packing them in tissue and dinky carrier bags. 'Must be nice to have that kind of dosh to spend,' I said.

'Money can't buy you style,' said Pia, but I knew she was only trying to make me feel better, because she added in a flat zombie voice. 'We-are-not-slaves-to-fashion.'

'Oh yes, we are!' I said. I whipped my jacket off and put it on back to front. I put my arms out straight in front of me, à la zombie, and began to stagger towards the shop next door. 'Must-have-new-clothes. Must-have-new-clo-othes,' I droned. Pia did the same with her jacket, putting her arms out in front of her and following me, doing a stiff shuffling walk as she went.

'Hey, Hall,' said a male voice behind us. I turned to see that it was Roy Mason from the Lower Sixth. Tom's classmate. He was with Josh Tyler and they were looking at us as if we were completely mad. I did a quick glance around. Luckily no sign of Tom. Phew. I so didn't want him to see me acting like an idiot. Doing the zombie shuffle is *not* a pulling technique I'd recommend. It was OK that Roy and Josh had seen me. Neither of them were on my boy wish list. Roy was blond, and nice enough looking, but he smelt like stale biscuits, and Josh was dark and stocky and way too touchy-feely – like he was always desperate for a grope.

I did my best snooty impersonation and looked down my nose at them. 'Queen of the Zombies, actually,' I said. 'Kneel and obey.'

Josh and Roy both stuck their arms out and started to do the zombie walk towards us. Josh even began dribbling. Eew. Typical. Boys always take it too far.

Josh lumbered over to me. 'Undead need warm flesh,'

he said, in a stupid droolie voice. 'Give me your arm.'
He bent over to bite my arm while sticking his nose a
little too near to my chest.

'In your dreams, Tyler,' I said and shoved him off.
Unfortunately, I caught him off balance and he stag-
gered towards Roy, lost his footing, toppled over and
landed with a thud just at the moment that Tom, my
love, keeper of my heart, stepped off the escalator. His
hair was windswept and he had on a black jacket and
jeans and looked every inch the teen movie star. He
saw Josh fall, glanced at me and raced over. 'You all
right, mate?' he asked Josh, who looked embarrassed
and scrambled quickly to his feet.

'Yeah, yeah,' he said. 'I was just telling Jess here that
I didn't fancy her. Some girls just can't take rejection.'

'As *if*,' I said. 'You are *so* not my type.' I turned to
Tom. It was the first time I'd seen him close up and now
I saw that he had beautiful jade-coloured eyes with
thick lashes and a gorgeous mouth with a plump
bottom lip. I had to drag my eyes away from it. 'I didn't
mean to shove him. We were being zombies. I'm Jess,
by the way.' My fantasy meeting with him flashed
through my mind. *What was it I was going to say to him?*
Oh yeah. 'I'm the school's best swimmer,' I blurted. *Oh*
noooo, I thought as soon as the words were out of my
mouth, *What have I said? I'm an idiot. Best swimmer!*
He'll think I'm a show-off . . . And what was I doing? Being

a zombie. He'll think I'm mad. And Josh falling over! Tom will think I'm a bully . . .

Pia made a nervous tittering sound and linked her arm through mine to pull me away. She'd sensed disaster with a capital D.

Tom looked at me as if I'd just escaped from a mental hospital. He clapped Josh on the shoulder and led him away with Roy, who was sniggering. As they walked off, without looking round, Josh lifted his right arm and stuck the middle finger of his hand up.

'Same to you,' I called and made a rude gesture back. Sadly it was Tom who turned round and saw it, not Josh. He gave me a filthy look.

'Oops,' I said and grinned like an idiot, then waved. *Waved!* What was I thinking?

Tom shook his head like he couldn't believe anyone as awful as me could possibly exist.

'Well, um . . . at least you've spoken to Tom now,' said Pia, as the boys disappeared round the corner.

'Yeah. Big introduction. So much for making a good first impression. I finally get to meet the coolest boy in school and he sees me acting as one of the undead. I was wearing my jacket back to front, for heaven's sake. Oh *God!* Talk about dressed to impress. Not. That couldn't have gone worse if I'd planned it.'

Pia squeezed my arm. 'Well, you did say you wanted him to notice you and um . . . well, he did. And um . . .

he will surely see that you're different.' She giggled. 'He's not going to forget you in a hurry.'

'No. I will probably appear in his nightmares eating warm flesh and crunching on eyeballs. Oh hell. Can this day get any worse?' My phone rang.

I glanced at the screen. Dad.

2

Nooooo!

'I don't want to go,' I said. 'Why do we have to live there?'

'Because you belong with your father,' said Gran, 'and this new job means that you can all be together.' She said it in her firm 'and-that's-the-end-of-that' voice, which didn't give away how she felt.

'Job as general dogsbody. It's not much of a promotion.' I knew I was being whiney and I don't normally do the sulk act but I couldn't help it.

We were sitting around the table having Sunday breakfast, a couple of weeks after the news that Dad had got the job. We being Gran, Charlie and my aunt Maddie, who had dropped by to stick her nose in. I was moaning because it was all feeling real now – Dad had started at Porchester Park on Friday and our moving-in date was all set.

'Some people don't *have* jobs,' Aunt Maddie said as she tucked into the scrambled eggs that Gran had made. 'Some people don't have *homes*. *Some* people don't even have water. You should be grateful.'

'Oo-er, get her,' I said. Aunt Maddie is so earnest about everything, always was, but more so since she met her new boyfriend, an Australian called Brian. Mr New Age Wonder from Down Under. Since she met him, she's forever going on about feeding the hungry, homing the homeless, changing the world. It's all very well but I don't *want* to change the world. I'm fourteen. I like the world how it is. I want to enjoy it, but Aunt Maddie always has to make me aware of the under-privileged and how we should all be doing more. Plus she's become vegetarian and gone green, stopped wearing make-up and had her lovely long hair cut into a shoulder-length bob that looks just like Gran's. I don't think it suits her shorter, it makes her look much older than her thirty-seven years. She could be a ten in the looks scale if she wanted. She and Charlie are like my mum and Gran, with their fine bone structure and honey-coloured eyes. I, on the other hand, am more like Dad, with his long nose and blue eyes. Aunt Maddie never had style, though, unlike Mum who had a great eye for making an outfit sassy and feminine. Gran has style too, but a different kind – more boho chic in her devore velvet tops and floaty scarves. Mum and her sister were such opposites. Aunt Maddie wears old jeans, T-shirts and fleeces. Fleeces! I remember

Mum messing about once and saying, 'Dahlings, always remember, wherever you are, you must *never* forget your sense of style.' She never did. She was forty when she died but she always looked younger, until the end that is, when she lost her hair because of the chemotherapy, but even then she made an effort. She bought some brightly-coloured velvet berets instead of doing the wig thing and she always looked good in them. She loved to dress up for glamour or fun – like when she came to the swimming events I competed in. She'd show up with a daft bathing cap on and make Charlie wear one too. I think people at our school thought she was mad. She was a bit. I wince now when I think how embarrassed I was when she first turned up in one of her crazy caps. Now I'd do anything to see her sitting on the benches at the pool looking like a prize eejit, complete with a bucket and spade.

Aunt Maddie used to join in too, if she was persuaded, but now it's like she's lost her sense of humour and become Miss Mega Intense. The first thing she does when she comes over is turn off the TV if it's on standby, switch off the lights, separate all Gran's rubbish into individual recycling bags, and then she lectures Gran about not buying enough wholewheat bread or organic food. I think it's insulting to Gran. It's her house, not Aunt Maddie's. Anyway, I was getting into all things green long before she began to hold the torch.

I got it. Planet in trouble. We need to act. I've been doing my bit. I recycle my computer printer cartridges, pass on my mags, helped make a compost bin in the garden . . . yet Aunt Maddie makes out like she's the only one who's ever had a green thought or given to charity and the rest of us are evil, materialistic, devil-worshipping consumers. People like her who go on and on about it and lay a guilt trip on everyone in sight bring out the worst in me and I do whatever I can to wind her up.

'Are you listening?' she asked.

'Yes, course. I was just thinking about the lack of water. I have a solution.'

'What?' asked Aunt Maddie.

'Dilute it,' I said. Only Gran laughed. 'And tonight, I hope we'll be having pasta so I can work on my carbonara footprint.' I cracked up at my own brilliant joke and again Gran laughed with me. Charlie groaned. Aunt Maddie rolled her eyes.

'I think you'll love the place once you get there,' said Gran, changing the subject, as always trying to keep the peace. Not that the subject of the move was much better.

'I doubt it,' I said. I'd seen the photos. Number 1, Porchester Park. It looked like a great concrete and glass tower. Really boring, with no history. I liked Gran's house, with its familiar clutter in every room, its old-fashioned marble fireplaces, the cornicing on the ceiling. It had been built in the Victorian era and I liked to lie on my bed sometimes and try and imagine the different families who had lived there before us. Once, when Gran was decorating, I helped her scrape the paint off a door in the hall and we went through about eight layers of it, down to a deep maroon colour. It was great to think that someone had put that paint there so many years ago; had actually chosen and applied that colour. After that, Gran and I got really into the history of the house and went on the net and looked up the names of the people who had first lived there. James Erstine, a solicitor, lived there with his wife Emma, his mother, Lily, and his three children – Rose, Estelle and baby Walter. I could almost picture them. I liked stuff like that, but there was going to be no chance of it in the new place. It was all brand spanking new.

'We'll see for ourselves soon enough,' said Charlie. 'Dad's coming to take us over there later.'

'And you won't have to change schools,' Gran added.

'Yeah, it'll just take me an eternity to get there, like a bus and a walk. I'll have to get up half an hour earlier.'

'Oh poor Jess,' said Aunt Maddie. 'In some countries, children have to go out and work at your age or younger.'

'Yeah, well, this isn't some country, this is England.

Get a grip, Aunt Maddie. And if you feel so bad about it, why don't *you* go and work in a third world country somewhere?'

'I might,' she said. 'But honestly, Jess, you should be supporting your dad, not giving him a hard time. It's a brilliant career opportunity for him at a time when work is scarce, so you should stop being selfish and acting like such a spoilt brat.'

As always, Charlie didn't taken sides. Instead, he picked up his guitar and started to strum it. Moments later, he began to sing. OK, so he has a good voice, but I hear too much of it, morning, noon and night.

Aunt Maddie started making coffee. She likes to make it from coffee beans which involves this little machine that grinds them down and makes a din. She'd given one to Gran last Christmas, so she could always have her coffee the way she liked it when she came round.

Gran cleared away the dishes and put on Radio Four.

Sunday breakfast with my family. The noise level is enough to drive a person mad.

I went up to my room, where Dave had cleverly escaped the pandemonium and was snoozing, a mass of black-and-white fur on the end of my bed. He opened one sleepy eye.

'All right, Dave?'

He meowed and lifted his nose as if to say, yeah.

I glanced at one of the photos on the bedside cabinet. It had been taken the Christmas before Mum got ill. It was of Mum, Charlie and me in front of the tree playing out another of Mum's dressing-up ideas. We were all wearing Santa hats, baubles as earrings and big grins.

What would you think about this move? I wondered as I looked at Mum. As if she had heard, one of the last things she'd said to me flashed into my mind. It had been about a week before the drugs she was on made her too sleepy to talk, and even then when she did say anything, she didn't always make sense, like she'd already gone into another world. This day, however, I'd been crying and she'd taken my hand and told me that she wanted me to promise not to waste time being miserable when she'd gone. 'Life's too short. I want you to be brave and to be happy, to have fun,' she had said, and then she'd smiled. 'Plus, frowning gives you wrinkles.'

'I suppose there's no getting out of the move,' I told the photo, 'so OK, for you, Mum, and so that I don't get any wrinkles, I'll try to be brave about it. Happy, I can't quite stretch to at the moment but I'll work on it.'

3

First Impressions

'Welcome to your new home!' said Dad.

Dad had picked up Charlie and me after breakfast to give us our first look at where we'd be living. Aunt Maddie had wanted to come too but, luckily for us, Brian was taking her off to some Hairy-Armpits-R-Us type demo in town.

I looked around Porchester Park's vast lobby, with its pale marble floors and ceiling height glass walls to the front and the back. *Hmm, cosy? Not.*

The front of the building looked out onto a covered, curved driveway and beyond that to a broad courtyard paved with black slate tiles. In the middle, on a plinth, was a polished bronze sculpture of what looked, to me, like an enormous bum. A bum about six foot wide. Not really my taste in art, though it looked expensive.

'Posh booty,' I whispered to Charlie and he laughed.

Through the back wall, I could see a garden with a tree overlooking a pool. I knew it was a maple from when Charlie was a boy scout, back in the days when he talked instead of sang. He was forever going on nature trails then and telling us what he'd seen at every opportunity. I pointed at the tree. 'Maple,' I said. 'Dib dib, dob dob, I know my trees.' Charlie smiled, but his face wasn't giving much away as he looked around.

Home is not a word I would use to describe this place, I thought, as I glanced over at Charlie. The place was smart, no doubt about it, but it looked cold and bland to me. In fact, it could have been an upmarket hotel lobby just about anywhere in the world.

A few men in smart suits like the one Dad was wearing hurried about looking important. One was talking into his mobile, another clutched a file in one hand. He glanced over at me and Charlie, probably wondering who these two scruffs were: Charlie in his ripped jeans and schizophrenic T-shirt (it says: 'I used to be schizophrenic, but we're OK now'), me in my jeans and blue tunic top.

'Of course, it will all come to life when the residents move in,' Dad enthused. 'There'll be a pyramid of fresh flowers every day and some fantastic artwork on the walls, a seating area over to your left, a uniformed doorman at the front and at least two parking valets, maybe three.'

'Um,' I managed to mumble. I didn't know what to say although *nooooooooooo*, came to mind. I'm really not sure how it's going to be, living with Dad again after six years apart. I reckon he's feeling much the same way, judging by his strained expression. Both of us seem on edge.

'Want to see our place first?'

Charlie and I shrugged and followed Dad through a tall smoked-glass door at the back.

'Conference rooms, the admin area, my office,' Dad pointed out as we followed him through a long wood-panelled corridor with closed doors on the right, through another door and eventually out into a back area. Five modern houses had been built around a paved courtyard with a giant palm tree in the middle. Dad took a key out of his pocket and opened the door of the second one along. 'This'll be us,' he said. 'I'll be moving in this week to get everything ready for when you two come and join me.'

Inside was just empty rooms, newly-painted if the smell was anything to go by. Upstairs were two medium-sized bedrooms and a bathroom and one smaller bedroom with its own en suite shower. All brand new and cream-coloured. Cream tiles, cream walls, cream carpets. *No character*, I thought. Gran's house is a riot of colour: deep red in the hall; turquoise in the bathrooms; yellow in the kitchen; woven rugs and artefacts on every surface.

'Which bedroom do you want? The smaller one with

its own en suite shower or the bigger one which has to share the bathroom with me?' asked Dad.

'What do you think?' I asked Charlie.

He shrugged. 'You take the one with the shower – as long as I can use it sometimes.' He knew I'd prefer that to sharing with Dad.

Downstairs was a featureless open-plan living room with a kitchen and breakfast bar at the back and a door that led out to the garden. Medium-sized. Same cream colour on the walls. Same cream stone tiles on the floor. All very clean, very boring. Through the back window, I could see a small patio area and a perfect lawn that ran thirty feet or so down to a large summerhouse with a porch in the corner. *At least Dave has some outside space*, I thought, as Dad explained that the summerhouse stored sunloungers for the residents to use.

'Although I am tempted to use it as an escape from work,' said Dad.

'What for?' I asked.

'Peace, pottering, my own space,' he replied.

Space away from us, I thought, wondering again why Dad was making us do all this, when he obviously preferred having time to himself.

We spent the next hour on a tour of the main building. 'Fifty apartments, six duplex penthouses . . .' Dad droned on, sounding exactly like an estate agent. We trudged after him down one long wood-panelled corridor after another, until we arrived at some lifts.

'Cedarwood,' said Dad, about the panelling.

Whatever, I thought. 'The decorators liked wood, didn't they?' I said. 'What do you call a man with a tree growing out of his head?'

'What?' Dad asked.

'Ed Wood. What do you call a man with *two* trees growing out of his head?'

Charlie rolled his eyes. 'Ed Woodward, and three trees would be Edward Woodward.'

Dad ignored us, and pressed the lift button to go up. 'These are for staff and deliveries,' he said. 'The lift for the residents is round the front.' It all felt so quiet, so lifeless. I couldn't imagine living in such a heartless place. I thought about what I'd be leaving behind. At Gran's house, there were books, paintings, things to do, people dropping by. It was lived in, as my mum used to say.

'So, what do you think?' asked Dad, as we stepped out after him onto the sixth floor and into yet another corridor.

'It's like a hotel,' I said. 'Anonymous.'

'Only in the public areas,' said Dad. 'We keep them neutral but inside, each apartment will be totally individual.'

I glanced at Charlie again. He wrinkled his nose. In

nose talk, that meant he was as unsure about the place as I was.

'And you say "hotel",' Dad continued, 'but actually it's a very different kind of place. These apartments will be people's homes, each one unique. Today's Sunday, so it's quiet, but you should have been here on Friday. It was like Piccadilly Circus. In fact, for the last nine months, the residents have had interior designers in practically non-stop, frantically remodelling their homes to make them into some of the most spectacular dwellings in London.'

'Can we see one?' I asked.

'No. There might still be people working in them,' said Dad as he pulled a key from his pocket. 'But I can show you one that hasn't been sold yet. I have the keys to number thirty. Maybe I can sneak you in to see one that's been refurbished later.'

'How much do they cost?' asked Charlie.

'I'll give you a clue,' Dad replied. 'The ones at the lower end start with a two and a five.'

'Two hundred and fifty thousand?' I said. 'That's pretty good for this area.'

Dad shook his head.

'Two million five hundred?' Charlie suggested. 'Awesome.'

'Wrong again,' said Dad, and he made a gesture with his hand to say that we should up our price.

'Twenty-five *million*. And that's just for starters. One of the penthouses just sold for ninety-four million.'

'What!?' Charlie and I chorused.

'No way,' said Charlie.

'Let's deffo have a look then,' I said. I tried to work out how many tops I could buy for that kind of money. Only about a billion trillion squillion.

'Why so much?' asked Charlie. 'This place is pretty cool but for that amount of dosh, it doesn't look so special.'

'Ah,' said Dad. 'Wait until you see inside. One of our residents is spending eight million on their apartment interior alone, plus this is the most prestigious postcode in London. Harrods and Harvey Nichols are a mere stone's throw away . . .'

I laughed. 'Cool. We can tell our mates at school that our corner shop is Harrods: "Just popping out for a pint of milk, Monty dahling."'

Dad laughed too and some of the tension I'd been feeling since we'd got here dissipated.

'And Sloane Street isn't far,' I added. 'Yummy scrum shops there.'

'And downstairs, there are plenty of car parking spaces,' continued Dad. 'Which is unusual, given that a single parking place round here can cost up to three hundred thousand pounds to buy.'

Charlie let out a low whistle. 'Mega bucks.'

Dad pointed at the floor. 'We have four hundred of them underneath here in the car park.'

'Aunt Maddie would have a heart attack,' I said.

'The main thing about this place, though, is that it's serviced. There are lots of apartment blocks all over the city but only a handful of them are serviced.'

'What does that mean?' I asked.

'It means it works like a hotel, which is probably why you thought it felt like one. We have our own staff here, but also work in tandem with those at the Imperial Lotus hotel next door. So we can use their kitchens and chefs, if, for example, a resident wants a banquet at midnight, or even something as simple as a sandwich. We can also use their laundry service twenty-four/seven if we need to.'

'Oh Jeeves, have my undies washed, pressed, sprayed with French perfume and brought up to my room,' I said in a posh voice.

Dad ignored me. 'All the apartments have their own kitchens and some residents travel with their own cooks,' he went on. 'My job is to ensure that whatever the residents want on top of what their own staff do, it's provided.'

'How much does that cost a year?' Charlie asked.

'The service charge? Around fifty thousand pounds,' said Dad. 'But sometimes it's not that much, as residents have so many of their own staff as well.

One's taken four apartments, two of which are just for his staff. He has thirty-five people in all, some of whom will live in, and others who'll live out in apartments nearby.'

'Thirty-five staff?' I asked. 'To do what?'

'Chef, laundry maid, PA, masseur, hairdresser, nanny, chauffeur, pilot . . . that sort of thing. Oh, and of course, bodyguards: there'll be quite a few of them around the place.'

'Quite right. I'll be bringing my own personal slaves with me, too,' I said.

'Is that right?' said Dad, as he put the key in a door. 'That's me and Charlie covered, then. Still want to take a look?'

I nodded. 'Duh,' I said.

'Here we are.' He beckoned us in. 'After you, Madam, Sir. And before you say that this is still like a hotel, Jess, you have to remember that what you're seeing is just the base. Most of the residents will rip out what's been installed by the developers and put in decor to suit their own taste.'

We followed Dad into a wide circular hallway done in marble, smoked glass and blonde wood. A short corridor led into a vast open-plan space that almost took my breath away.

'Wow,' Charlie and I chorused.

Natural light poured through the double height floor-to-ceiling glass walls, giving a panoramic view over Hyde Park. The empty room felt like it was suspended in space.

'As I said,' said Dad. 'A blank canvas.'

'This room is the size of a tennis court,' said Charlie, as he crossed the highly-polished floor to look out at the view of the park spread below us.

'I'd love to see what whoever buys it does with it,' I said as I went to join him. 'This is like looking out over the world. It's amazing. Like the entire park is your back garden.'

We gazed out over the trees and the loops of the River Thames winding away into the distance.

'You'd never think you were in a city,' said Charlie, 'it'd be great to sit out here and just watch it all.'

'And it must be magical at night,' I said as Dad opened the doors out onto the terrace that ran the length of the apartment.

Dad nodded. 'Particularly on the side which looks out over the city. The glass is light-sensitive. It darkens at night so that although you can see out, no-one can see in.'

The view was even better out on the terrace, where steps led up to a decked area with a small pool.

'Hot tub for watching the stars,' said Dad. 'One of the penthouse suites even has its own infinity pool up on the roof.'

'Heaven. When can I move in?' I asked.

Dad smiled and beckoned us back inside. 'Look in the bedroom.'

We followed him into a vast bedroom on the other side of the apartment where we saw the familiar view of Harrods in the distance and Harvey Nichols to the left.

'Awesome,' I said. 'Town *and* country depending which way you're looking, though I guess the apartments on the lower floors don't have such great views.'

'It's amazing the cutting-edge technology these apartments have – walk-through, heat-activated lights, surround-sound,' Dad continued in his role as tour guide. 'You can choose the music when you come in and have it follow you around from room to room, and many of the residents will have their own private cinemas.'

'Wowza,' called Charlie from behind us. 'Check out this bathroom, Jess.'

I went to join him and gasped. The bathroom was bigger than Gran's living room. A single sheet of pale rose marble covered the floor, a darker marble – the colour of blue ink – was on the wall and two floor-to-ceiling mirrors made the room look as if it went on forever. It felt surreal as I looked at repeat images of myself receding into the distance.

Dad tapped his foot on the floor. 'They used the finest marble. Rose aurora from Portugal. Costs a fortune.'

'And you say some people will actually rip this *out*?'
I asked.

Dad shrugged. 'If it's not to their taste.'

'So if a resident's redecorating, it'd be a good day to look in the skips around here,' Charlie commented.

'It would,' said Dad. 'Only their decorators don't do skips.'

'Shame,' said Charlie.

'What sort of people are going to live here?' I asked.

'All sorts. It'll be international – Germans, Russians, Americans, Arabs, Japanese, Italians, Indians, you name it . . .'

'Martians?' asked Charlie.

'Maybe a few of those, too,' said Dad. 'If they can afford it.'

'Rich folk,' said Charlie.

'*Very* rich folk,' agreed Dad. 'Some of the richest in the world.'

'I can't wait to see in some of the apartments that *have* been done,' I said.

'They are out of this world but you have to remember that most of the residents have bought here for privacy, so I can't really show you around.'

'Oh please, Dad. *Please*. Just a peek.'

Dad laughed and shook his head. 'The security system here was created by the SAS. It's presidential standard – panic rooms, bullet-proof windows . . .'

Charlie whistled. 'Impressive.'

'It's virtually impossible to get into – and you want me to let *you* have a nose around?' Dad continued.

I nodded. 'Yep.'

For a brief second, Dad looked like a naughty boy. 'I'll see what I can do. Maybe once. Just *once*. Now. Where else? On the fifth floor is a hospitality suite with a bar and an outside terrace for when any of the residents wish to entertain outside of their home, but the decorators have been in there today and the walls and doors are probably still wet. So – how about the spa?'

'There's a spa? Cool,' I said.

He took us down to the ground floor and through to the back, where a whole area was hidden behind a tall sanded glass partition. Down some steps and through a small reception room was an Olympic-size swimming pool, the bottom of which was made up of different-coloured blue and turquoise mosaic tiles. I couldn't help but grin.

'You left the best to last,' I said.

Dad looked puzzled. 'Why's that?'

I pointed at my chest. 'Championship swimmer. Remember?'

Dad hesitated and a look of concern flashed over his face. 'Of course, er . . . let's get on, shall we?' He led us through another door into a large airy gym. It was Charlie's turn to perk up.

'All the latest equipment. Treatment rooms, a sauna, jacuzzi, steam room,' Dad continued. 'At the back there are two all-weather tennis courts and behind that some squash courts.'

It was too much to take in, but what I did get was that I, Jess Hall, would be living in the tip top topper-most of Poshville. I couldn't *wait* to tell Pia all about it.

By the time Dad dropped me at Pia's house later that afternoon, my mind was buzzing with possibilities. What colour to do my room. What posters to put on the walls. How to make the bland house we were going to live in more homely. And that gorgeous pool. I could swim every morning without having to get a bus! Bliss and a half.

Pia lived in an end-of-terrace house with a garden that overlooked cricket grounds at the back. I loved going there. Her mum ran a mini health centre from their home and she really knew how to create a peaceful atmosphere – like no matter what mood you arrived in, part of you went 'Ahhhh!' as soon as you walked through their front door. It always smelt divine – from the lavender and rose oils that Pia's mum burnt in the hall – plus the house had been feng shui-ed, so it had a good vibe and was painted in soft pastel colours that were easy on the eye. Mrs Carlsen had done loads of different courses and could do every type of massage going: from Indian to Swedish to sports. She gave me a head massage once after Mum died and it was pure heaven, even though I did cry my eyes out halfway through. My defence of being tough and coping just crumbled, partly because I suddenly realised that I would never experience the soothing touch of my mum's hands again and partly because Mrs Carlsen had a knack of getting at whatever's bothering a person. She's a force to be reckoned with, is Pia's mum, and I'm slightly intimidated by her. I'm also scared that somehow she'll get my biggest secret out of me when my defences are down, the one that I've never told anyone, not even Pia. Mrs Carlsen is mega together – the sort of person who makes the most of things, gets stuff done and asks exactly what she wants to know, which can be difficult if you have something to hide and she gets you in her radar. She'd have been a great policewoman getting criminals to confess – but then she'd be good at anything, really, if she set her mind to it.

Pia says that business hasn't been good lately, though – people are cutting back and luxuries like being pampered are one of the first things to go. Her mum still has her regular clients, but they visit her once a month now, instead of once a week like they used to.

Pia's worried that her mum won't be able to keep paying the rent and that they might have to move to somewhere cheaper when the lease is up for renewal, and her mum might even have to look for a new career. I was sure that Mrs Carlsen would come up with some plan or other but it made me realise how selfish I'd been, objecting so much to the move away from Gran's – at least my dad had a job and we'd have a secure home. *Uber-secure*, I thought, when I remembered that the SAS had created the security system.

'Hey,' said Pia, as we went through to the kitchen. 'Mum found an article about that place you're moving into in one of the supplements today.'

'Really? What did it say?'

'Apparently Jefferson Lewis is moving there.'

'Jefferson Lewis, the actor?'

'Yup. And his family.'

'Really? Dad never told me.' Jefferson Lewis was a mega Hollywood star, one of the most famous and highly-paid African-American actors in the world. I'd seen all his movies.

'That's what it said,' said Pia. 'Him and his family.' She rummaged through a pile of papers and found the magazine. 'Here it is: "Jefferson Lewis will be moving to Number 1, Porchester Park, the new luxury apartment block in Knightsbridge. It will be home to the elite – oil barons, oligarchs, Saudi princes and A-list stars."'

'What's an oligarch?' I asked.

'I wondered that. I asked Mum. She said it's a wealthy businessman who has a lot of political influence and is part of the government. I think she said they're Russian. Something like that.'

'Oligarch. Sounds like a character out of *Lord of the Rings*,' I said, 'or some weird fairy tale. Like, the fairies live on the top floor, the elves on the fourth floor, third floor is the giants and trolls, second floor, the oligarchs.'

Pia laughed and flicked through the magazine, then pointed to a photo of Jefferson Lewis with a woman and two teenagers: a boy who looked about seventeen and a girl of about our own age.

'"Jefferson Lewis with his wife Carletta, son Jerome, and daughter Alisha",' read Pia. 'Jerome's handsome, isn't he?'

I glanced at the picture and nodded. 'He looks cool and Alisha is pretty.'

Pia continued reading. '"Jefferson Lewis is over here working on his new film, *Time After Time*, but has told the press that he would like a permanent base here in the UK."' Pia glanced up at me and grinned. 'Excellent.'

I grinned back. 'Yeah. Maybe.' *Hmm*, I thought. *Maybe life at the new block isn't going to be quite so boring after all.*

4
The Price of Fame

'I have to sign on your behalf and I . . . um, I'm sure you don't, but I have to ask, check, that is, that neither of you have . . . er, a criminal record,' said Dad. Charlie and me had been back at school a few days and Dad had dropped in on Wednesday evening to go over a few details about the move in just over two weeks' time.

Gran burst out laughing.

'What? Like are we international drug dealers or shoplifters?' asked Charlie.

'No – yes, that sort of thing. Nonsense, I know, but everyone who is going to work or live at Porchester Park has to be checked by the Criminal Records Bureau,' said Dad. He shifted in his chair and looked embarrassed about having asked us.

'Oh, Michael, you surely know your own kids well enough to know the answer,' said Gran.

Dad smiled, but he looked strained. He often did when he was round at Gran's. I think he was intimidated by her, probably because Gran had always felt that Mum and Dad should have stuck with their marriage. She often said her generation didn't do divorce.

I felt for Dad, so decided to try and lighten the situation. 'What about that time you wore those purple velvet jeans, Charlie?' I said. 'I'd call those criminal. Write that down, Dad. I think the residents at the new block need to be warned about Charlie's dress sense, or rather lack of it.'

'You can talk!' Charlie replied.

'At least I wear jeans that fit me. The crotch on yours is down by your knees and they're so low on your hips that most days you can see your underwear. Yeah, Dad, warn the residents. Bum alert. Son of manager is likely to do a moonie at any moment.'

Dad laughed, then glanced at Gran. 'Yes, well – although there's no dress code as such, you must be reasonably smart. Also . . . I'm sure there's no real need for this but I need to remind you of the responsibility you, we – as a family – will be taking on with this new position. I must insist that you keep and respect the privacy of the residents.'

'Yes, of course,' I blurted. Probably a bit too quickly and I hoped that Dad didn't see me blush. News that I was going to be moving to Poshville had spread round school like a Chinese whisper, getting more and more outrageous as it travelled. Leonardo di Caprio was going to be a resident. Prince Charles. A couple of African princes. Top film directors. Billionaire rock stars . . . Yet, even though those particular people wouldn't be living there, the rumours weren't actually that far from the truth. And I was enjoying the attention. I couldn't help it. The fact that I would be living in close proximity to people with mega bucks was too good not to share. People were well impressed. The move was giving me kudos. I'd even noticed Tom checking me out one morning at break when I was talking to Charlie, although I suppose he might have been looking to see if I was going to go into my Zombie Queen routine again.

'But . . . um, Dad, sometimes people just find out things,' I continued. 'Like Pia read about the Lewises in the paper.'

'Of course,' said Dad. 'And that's fine. Just don't go giving people any gossip yourselves, that's all I'm saying.'

Shame, I thought. I'd been enjoying my new-found status as celebrity co-habitee.

The next day, at school, I found out just how hard it was going to be not to talk about the apartment block. My mates, Flo and Meg, were straight onto it. Pia and I often hang out with them and have regular sleepovers and I tell them about most things that are happening to me – apart from my secret about Mum's funeral. I still can't bring myself to talk to anyone about that.

'Hey, Jess, is it true that you're going to be living in the same place as Tom Cruise?' asked Flo as she wound her long golden hair back into a clip.

'And Kylie, I heard that Kylie will be living there,' said Meg. She was wide-eyed at the idea, because she'd done an impersonation of Kylie at the end-of-term concert last year and everyone had said how much she looked like her – petite, pretty and blonde.

We're an odd-looking bunch of friends, really. Flo and I are tall, Meg and Pia are five inches smaller. And we have such different styles: like Flo is such a girlie girl, willowy and sugar sweet, wearing floaty tops in all shades of pink outside of school. Meg would gag if she had to wear pink. She's more of a tomboy and lives in jeans and sneakers and is sports mad. We'd love to do a makeover on her and get her into a dress but, knowing her, she'd wear it with boys' boots to make a point. Pia's style is a mix of vintage and retro, and she often wears ethnic jewellery or a big flower brooch. And I like indie. Still, it doesn't matter *what* we look like, the main thing is, we get on and we have a laugh most days.

In response to Meg's comment, I shrugged a shoulder like I was oh so cool. 'Kylie? Maybe. I'm not allowed to say.'

'Oh, come on, Jess. We're your mates, we won't tell,' pleaded Flo.

'If I told you, I'd have to kill you,' I said.

'And if she doesn't, one of the bodyguards will,' Pia added as Chrissie Alberg and Sophie James from Year Ten sidled over to join us. 'One family who's going to live there has *eight* bodyguards.'

'That's probably Tom Cruise,' said Chrissie. 'I read somewhere that he has a huge entourage.'

'So what's it like there?' asked Sophie.

The words *big, cold and bland* came to mind, although I'd only seen the one apartment, not that I was going to let on about that. 'Imagine your most fabulous fantasy house,' I replied, 'then quadruple it.'

'Awesome,' said Flo. She was a total romantic and loved a fantasy of any kind. She read nothing else and her bedroom was done out with posters from *Lord of the Rings* and *Eragon*. I think she secretly fancied herself as an elfin princess.

'Truly,' I said.

'Last week, Jess had to give her fingerprints,' said Pia as the crowd of girls around us grew, 'and someone has been round to take photos of her and Charlie's eyes. The security system was designed by the SAS.'

'Eyes?' asked Sophie. 'Why?'

'Their irises,' Pia continued. 'People can fake loads of

things but it's virtually impossible to copy someone's iris, isn't that right, Jess?'

'Er—' I started.

But Pia was on a roll. You'd have thought *she* was the one moving into Porchester Park.

'When you pass from the staff living area into the main building,' Pia confided, 'a secret face recognition camera scans your eyes to make sure that it's really you.'

'Wow,' said Meg. 'That's cool.'

I pinched Pia to try and get her to shut up. What she'd just revealed was exactly the sort of thing Dad wouldn't want being repeated.

She winced. 'Ow! What did you do that for?'

I put my finger up to my lips to say *be quiet*, but it was too late, our audience was captivated.

'I suppose that they have to be careful in case anyone captures you, clones you, then poses as you and tries to kidnap one of the mega richies,' said Flo.

I rolled my eyes. 'Yeah, right. That'd be it.'

'It does happen,' insisted Chrissie.

'Yeah just like that time the aliens captured you and ate your brain,' I said as I pulled Pia away. Not to be left out, Meg and Flo followed after us.

'No need to be sniffy,' called Sophie. 'Just because you're living there doesn't mean you're one of them.'

I was about to put her right and rub in the fact that I *would* be one of them actually, because I'd be living there and my dad was the general manager, but I remembered what Dad had said so I bit my tongue.

'Why did you pinch me?' asked Pia as we turned a corner in the corridor.

'Because we – I – have to be discreet.'

'Since when? You've been telling everyone since we got back to school.'

'I have not!'

'You so have.'

'Not.'

'Have.'

'Not – OK. So maybe I have, but it has to stop. Part of living there is being private about it. Like the residents don't want anyone talking about them or discussing their lives.'

'She's right,' said Meg, and Flo nodded too. 'A-listers want privacy.'

Pia looked hurt. 'Yeah, I can understand that but it's *you* who's been talking about it so much, Jess.'

'I know, but Dad came round last night and told me and Chaz to keep it zipped.'

'But you'll always tell me, won't you?' asked Pia.

'And us,' chorused Meg and Flo.

I hesitated and an expression of hurt flashed over Pia's face. 'I don't know if I'll be able to,' I said. 'My life's not going to be like it was any more.' Images of the pool, the parties, the glamorous get-togethers to come flashed before my eyes. No doubt about it. I would be mixing with a very different set of people.

'I'll be able to come and see you there, won't I?' asked Pia.

'And us,' said Meg, with a nod to Flo.

'I don't know. I thought so, but now I don't know. All I know is that I'm not allowed to talk about it.'

Pia went quiet for a few moments and chewed her bottom lip like she was biting back tears. 'Not even to me?' she said finally.

Meg and Flo exchanged looks then linked their arms through Pia's.

'Oh God, I'm sorry. I didn't mean to upset you, P. Things are going to be different, that's for sure, I just don't know how much yet. We'll still see each other at school and I'll still be able to come to your house.'

'Yes, but are you going to want to? Like, if you're going to be mixing with glamorous people, like genuine celebrities, you might find me boring or start changing the rules like just now – telling me to shut up for talking about the place when I didn't know not to.'

'Hey, that's not fair.'

'Yes, it is. One day you're basking in it, telling everyone, and we're all in it together. Next day it's totally hush hush, but you haven't told me that things have changed. Best friends are supposed to tell each other everything, you know.'

Meg and Flo nodded. It felt like they'd all taken sides against me and I was the bad guy. I wanted to hit them.

'I do. I *will*.'

'But you just said you might not be able to tell me about what goes on in your life any more.'

'I . . . Oh, I don't know, Pia. Let's not row. I just don't know how it's going to be, that's all.'

The bell rang to say that break was over and as we made our way to our next class, Pia stayed linked with Meg and Flo and no-one linked with me, like they usually did. The atmosphere between us all was heavy. I felt bad. Pia was right. Up until now we had shared just about everything – from boy fantasies to lipgloss, music, mags, our hopes and fears, ambitions, hang-ups . . . And now she was upset with me. I ought to have been more sensitive. I knew things had been tough for her at home as it was tight on the dosh front for her and her mum. It can't have been easy hearing all about me getting ready to move into La-di-dah Land, where people have money falling out of their pockets. Knowing what to say and what not to say was difficult! Meg and Flo had clearly taken Pia's side, and Sophie blooming James had accused me of being sniffy; all because I didn't want to talk about where I'd be living. A card that Gran had pinned on the noticeboard in her kitchen flashed into my mind. It said, *some days the windscreen, some days the bug*. Now I knew what it meant.

5

Moving On

'OK, got everything?' asked Gran.

'Yup,' said Charlie.

It was a grey and blustery Sunday morning and we'd been up for hours, ready to go to our new home.

I nodded. 'Just got to get Dave. I've put him in the front room. When Dad's finished packing the car, I'll put him in the cat basket.'

'Good plan,' said Gran. 'Now, I've got a little something for each of you.'

She bustled off back to the kitchen, leaving Charlie and me in the hall with all our boxes and bags. I felt like I was going to cry and let out a long sigh. Charlie turned on me immediately.

'You've got to hold it together, Jess,' he said. 'Gran's been putting on a brave face all morning and if she sees you getting upset, it'll finish her off. She was close to tears last night when she was making dinner. She swore it was the onions, but I knew it wasn't.'

I sniffed back a sob. From the look on Charlie's pale face, he was giving himself a talking-to as much as me. Poor Charlie. I knew he missed Mum every bit as much as I did and this move was taking him away from familiar territory in just the same way as it was taking me. Gran's house hadn't just been a home, somewhere to stay; it had been a link with Mum, our childhood and happier times. Charlie was right. I had to keep it together or it would be Blub City round here.

'I'm fine,' I said. 'It's going to be great. A new chapter.'

Charlie squeezed my arm. 'Good girl.'

He picked up a box to take out to the car and Gran came back and handed me two torches. 'One for you, one for Charlie,' she said.

'Oh. OK, thanks,' I said. I didn't want to appear ungrateful but her gift made me laugh. I don't know what I'd been expecting – maybe a photo or one of her paintings – but definitely not a torch.

'Hey! You can never have too many torches,' she said. 'You never know when one might come in handy.'

'Exactly, Gran,' I said with a grin and switched mine on and held it under my chin like we did at Halloween to make ourselves look spooky.

It didn't take long to pack the car and as soon as I had Dave in the cat basket, we were ready to get on our way.

51

Gran gave me a huge hug and the familiar rose scent of her made me want to cry again. She felt so safe and solid. She let me go, pushed me towards the car and, when I was in the back seat, handed the cat basket in to me. Dave looked most put out, probably thinking cat baskets meant the vet's, and howled his objections loudly, which made us all laugh. I felt like he was crying for all of us as we tried to stay brave and cheery.

As we drove away, I turned back to wave to Gran and then my eyes did fill up. She looked as if someone had let the air out of her. Her shoulders had sagged and her figure was stooped, but she immediately stood up when she saw me looking back and waved until we turned the corner. Sometimes I wished things could always stay the same. This last year I was finding out fast that was not the way life goes. Things change constantly and you just have to go with it, whether you like it or not.

Choose, I thought. *I can sink or swim – and I choose to swim.*

I made myself sit up straight. 'So, Dad, what happens when we get there?'

As we left the familiar roads near Gran's, Dad drove along the King's Road, turned left at Sloane Square and went up Sloane Street, past Prada, Armani, Jimmy Choo, Dior, Gucci, Dolce & Gabbana and then up to

Knightsbridge. I knew all the shop names from Mum's magazines but had never been in any of them. Hovering at the entrance of most of them were big black men in dark suits and shades, wearing earpieces. They radiated an aura that said, 'Don't even *think* of coming in here if you need to ask the price of anything.'

'They're like bouncers at a nightclub,' said Charlie as he glanced out at them.

'Definitely not to be messed with,' I said as I watched one say something into his walkie-talkie. 'Though he's probably just calling his wife to say, "Emergency, I need chips and egg for me tea and a packet of HobNobs."'

'Or maybe he's calling his mate in the next-door shop, saying, "I'm bored out of my mind – let's pretend we're in a Bond movie. Bagsy I be 007."'

Dad looked over. 'Yeah,' he said. 'They're probably pussycats underneath.'

Yeah right, I thought as we took a left turn and headed along towards Number 1, Porchester Park. *Pussycats with sharp claws*. Somehow I didn't think I'd be checking those particular shops out any time soon.

The rest of the week flew by. I was busy at school, then my evenings passed at the house, in a haze of unpacking and rearranging. Dad had moved in the previous week, so had stocked the fridge and kitchen cupboards, put curtains up and even bought flowers for the living room – some white tulips – which I thought was a nice touch.

Pia came over to help on the first Saturday morning after we'd moved in. We'd soon made up after our blip. I'd apologised straight after class and promised her that I would always tell her everything. She was quick to forgive and when Meg and Flo saw that we were mates again, they dropped the cool act too. One thing that Mum drummed into me before she died was not to waste time when it came to people I cared about and to always say sorry if I'd upset anyone, because life was too short. So that's what I did. Anyway, Pia and I could never stay mad at each other for long. When I'd asked Dad about her coming to visit, he'd said that it would be fine as long as she phoned just before she arrived so I could let her in the side entrance. In the end, she'd arrived at Porchester Park first thing in the morning, so Dad had greeted her and brought her up to my room.

I had a present waiting for her. I'd been working on it all week. It was a compilation of songs by our favourite girl singers. I knew she'd love it because we were always swapping tracks we liked, so I knew just who her current faves were. I'd wrapped the CD up in silver paper tied with a pink ribbon, so it looked pretty. As soon as she came in, I handed it to her.

'To say I'm sorry again for being such a pigolette that day and that I can't imagine doing anything without you and that I hope you'll always be my best friend,' I said.

Pia smiled. 'Thanks, Jess, but that day is ancient history – forgotten.' She took the CD then reached into her bag and pulled out a similarly-packaged present. 'This is for you. A house-warming gift.'

I quickly unwrapped it. It was a scented candle. 'Perfect,' I said and gave her a hug.

'Mum says that it's important to get a house smelling the way you want it as quickly as possible.'

I sniffed the candle. It smelt divine. Spicy and sweet.

I showed Pia around and she looked impressed, even though it was an ordinary house. I wished I could show her the real Poshville and apologised that I couldn't take her into the main area without Dad being around. After he'd let Pia in, he'd gone for the day because some of the residents were due to arrive the following week and he was busy, busy, busy.

'It's not my dream house,' I said to Pia, after we'd done the tour and had gone into the garden, 'but I reckon we can make it nice. Dad said I can redecorate my room and do it whatever colour I want.'

'Least you've *got* a house,' she said. 'I don't know what Mum and I are going to do when the lease is up on the one we're in now.'

I squeezed her arm. 'Your mum will sort something. She always does.'

Pia smiled wistfully. 'Yeah. Maybe. Yeah. Course she will. At least we have until the end of November to find somewhere else. Maybe we'll buy one of the apartments here, hey? What are they? Only twenty million?'

'Yeah. Cheap at the price!'

'In that case, we may even buy two, dahling. One for each of us. What does Charlie think of the place?'

'I've no idea. He's the usual Charlie. Unfazed. He bounces along in his own little bubble. He's out today with his band. He just dumped his stuff, hung up a few clothes and that was it. Done. Moved in. Moved on. If he has any feelings about it, he'll probably write about it in one of his songs. Me, I want to get the house feeling cosy. I want to get cushions in and put my pictures up otherwise I think it looks too bland, too new.'

'I like it,' said Pia. 'And although it's not as big as your gran's, you do have all the perks of the complex.'

'Exactly,' I said. 'Swimming pool, spa, fab new people.' I saw Pia flinch, and I grabbed her hand and gave it a squeeze. 'More friends for *both* of us. Dad says that some of the families have kids. As well as the Lewis family, there's a Japanese family coming, they have two girls, I think. And a French couple. They sound interesting. Dad says that the man is an art dealer. There's also a

Russian family, though I can't remember if they have children. Um . . . and an American lady. She sounds old, family in banking etcetera and also – tadah, drum roll, though we mustn't tell anyone else – a Saudi family – royalty – *and* they have a son so I'll get to know a real prince!'

'Royalty! Wow,' said Pia. 'Cool.'

'I know. There'll be loads of new people because there are about fifty apartments up there. I've decided to be really positive about this move, you know. I'll get to know them, make friends. It'll be fab. Different, but fab and I'll share it all with you, you do know that, don't you?'

'Course,' Pia replied. 'Friends for life.'

'For richer for poorer, etcetera.'

'Exactly.'

We headed inside and I closed the back door behind us. I looked through the window over the sink back out at the empty garden. 'We *really* need to plant some stuff. Maybe we could do it together? Dad said that one of the staff gardeners would help, but I'd rather do it myself. Gran said she'd bring some cuttings from her garden to get things started and Dad says we can go to the garden centre to get some pots for the patio and some pansies to give it a bit of colour. It certainly needs it on a grey day like this.'

Pia shrugged. Gardening wasn't really her thing, but

I knew she'd help if she thought it would make me feel better about the move.

We went back up to my bedroom, where Dave was settled on the window ledge looking out. He'd been very unhappy about being cooped up and had spent most of his time with his paws up on the window peering out. I knew that he was dying to go outside but I couldn't let him – not for a good few weeks – in case he went wandering or tried to find his way back to Gran's house. He kept giving me terrible looks like he hated me and whenever I came into a room, he'd turn his back on me like it was my fault and he was saying, *I'm not your friend any more*. Pia went over to stroke him and he nuzzled her hand with his nose.

'He probably thinks that if he's nice to you, you'll sneak him out,' I said. 'But you're not leaving me, Dave, you hear?'

He ignored me and purred loudly at Pia's attentions.

'How many staff houses are there?' she asked as she looked out of the window.

'Five. I haven't met any of the neighbours yet. We're going to meet some of the people who work here tonight. Dad's asked everyone to a meeting at six to go over things and he said he'll introduce us then, although I've met a few of them just walking about the place—'

'Oh!' Pia suddenly stepped back from the window and hid behind the curtain.

'What?'

'Boy. Down there. I think he saw me.'

I went over to the window and looked down. A good-looking boy with shaggy dark hair, dressed in jeans and a red T-shirt, was going into the house next door. He glanced up, saw me and waved. I waved back.

'Who's he?' asked Pia.

'I don't know,' I said.

'Cute.'

'He's OK, not my type. Looks like a rugby player, stocky. I like slimmer boys like Tom.'

'Good,' said Pia, and she moved out from behind the curtain. 'Because I think he's Mr Hunky McFunky.'

I glanced down at him. He was still looking up with a cheeky grin on his face.

I laughed. 'Now you really *do* have a good excuse to come visit, P.'

She blushed. 'OK, here's your homework: Find out who he is. What star sign, what he's like and . . . if he has a girlfriend.'

I saluted her. 'Sometimes you are just like your mother. Mission received and understood. Will do.'

I looked down again. The boy had gone. He'd looked about Charlie's age, maybe older.

'Nice to know there'll be someone around our age as a neighbour,' I said.

Pia didn't answer. She was still peeping out from

behind the curtain, trying to see into next-door's front room.

The staff get-together was held up in the party room on the fifth floor of the complex. I'd been looking forward to having my irises scanned as we went through but Dad said that the security system wouldn't be up and running until next Monday, so we still had a week to move about freely. I took every opportunity to do so after Pia had gone home, and had a good explore as far as I could, although Dad had shown us most of it already.

As I wandered around, I met a few more of the staff. They were already in their places, even though the residents hadn't arrived yet. I wrote notes so that I could remember everyone – plus give Pia, Meg and Flo the lowdown at school on Monday.

Jacob: Gym. Dutch but no accent. Blond, slim, muscly, tanned with blue eyes. Early thirties?

Poppy Harrington: Spa. Forties? Ex-model, fab figure, long dark hair worn tied up.

Poppy was friendly and spoke with a posh accent. She made me a cup of green tea (Yuck. I tried to drink it, but it tasted of grass.) She asked a lot of questions about Dad. I wondered if she fancied her chances with him. Since Mum, Dad hadn't had a girlfriend, at least not one that Charlie or I knew about. I liked Poppy. I reckoned we could be friends and thought that I might encourage her and Dad by inviting her over. It would be fun to play Cupid.

Doormen: Didier – tall, handsome French man with a big smile, Yoram, an Israeli – Charlie says he's ex-army. Not very friendly.

You can see by the muscles on both their arms and their chests that these two are not to be messed with – although they look a lot more approachable than the doormen outside the shops on Sloane Street.

Reception: a beautiful Indian girl called Sita, and Grace – tall, blonde and a bit scary and efficient-looking.

In the evening, at Dad's request, Charlie and I got smartened up. For Chaz that meant jeans that weren't falling off him and abandoning his usual hoodie for a T-shirt. I, on the other hand, made a big effort and wore my red camisole and short cardi, black skirt and boots.

We hadn't seen the hospitality suite before and when we got there, it was way stylish. There was a small lobby near the lift which was similar in style to the Reception area downstairs. It opened through tall doors into the main room and at the back was a gleaming glass and chrome bar where a dozen stools covered in zebra-skin were lined up. On the bar were several bottles of wine, some cartons of juice and a few bowls of crisps for people to help themselves to, so Charlie and I went over to get a glass of apple juice.

Charlie went into a brill imitation of Dad and pointed at the walls. 'Covered with plum leather and silver suede,' he said then pointed to some modern sofas next to the gold armchairs. 'The slim sofas you see there are Italian – only the best, you know – and have been positioned next to those gold armchairs to provide contrast. New and old. It's the latest look. The chairs are antique. Worth a fortune, of course.'

I cracked up. I hadn't heard him do his imitation of Dad for a long time.

'As you can see, it's a big space, so it has been sectioned off with black wrought iron and opaque glass screens to provide our residents with private seating areas.' Charlie continued in Dad-speak as we looked around.

'Good for sneaky snogging,' I added.

'Our residents do not snog, madam, far too common,' said Charlie, still in his daft voice. He pointed up at the ceiling and continued. 'Overhead a fluted silver rotunda holds the hundred mini lights that softly illuminate the room.'

'Cost a fortune,' we said at the same time, then laughed.

Actually, it really was impressive, particularly when someone pressed a button somewhere and the floor-to-ceiling glass doors slid open to reveal a terrace that stretched almost the width of the entire building. There were enormous pots with palm plants out there and it looked very sophisticated, especially because it was night-time and there was a fab view of the city twinkling away in the distance.

Everyone was chatting and having a jolly old time getting to know each other, though no-one looked like they'd dressed up that much, even though Dad had made us make an effort. We'd only been there a short while when Dad called for silence and introduced me and Charlie. It was so embarrassing. I'm not normally a blusher but I could feel myself going as red as my top as they all turned to look at us.

'As for the rest of you,' said Dad, 'most of you already know each other but for those who don't, when I call your name, please make yourselves known. Don't worry if you can't place everyone this evening – it will all fall into place, I promise. There are lists at the door for you to take away with you, saying who's who, what they do and how you can all contact each other.'

I tried to remember everyone as their name was called out but there were too many of them and I had left my notebook back at the house. The gathered crowd soon became a blur of names and faces. Marguerite, who would be general housekeeper in charge of a team of cleaners and laundry people. Trevor, who would look after the underground garage and fleet of cars. Katie, Richard and Agnes who were hairdressers – and then

63

Katie's sister, Nicky, and her team of manicurists as well as beauticians, accountants, secretaries, valets, mechanics, porters, personal trainers, gardeners, chefs. The list went on and on. They seemed to be from all nations: Poland, Cyprus, Greece, India, Italy, Israel, France, the UK . . . I tried to remember where everyone was from but in the end there were just too many names and places to remember. Most of them wouldn't be living on-site – like the girls doing the beauty treatments, who would live nearby and just be on call. Others were based at the Imperial Lotus hotel next door, coming to Porchester Park as required. I looked for the cute boy Pia and I had seen, but couldn't see him anywhere. Maybe he had known that he would be introduced and made to look like an idiot, so had wisely opted out.

'Did you get who'll actually be living in the staff houses?' I asked Charlie as we made our way back to our house.

'That tall dark woman—' Charlie started.

'Poppy. She looks after the spa,' I said.

'Yeah. Her. Didier and Yoram have one of the smaller houses each. Then there's us, and Trevor who does the cars. All the rest of the staff live out. Apparently a lot of them are in another apartment block nearby or living locally.'

'So who's the boy I saw today, I wonder?'

Charlie shrugged, as if to say he didn't know, then

glanced down at the list that he'd picked up when we'd left the meeting. 'One hundred and forty-four staff,' he commented.

'And Dad says that most of the residents have their own staff living with them on top of that. Most travel with their own chef, nanny, PA, hairdresser or whatever.'

'Different world, hey?'

'I guess,' I said. 'But one I think I could get used to.'

After I'd emailed Pia, Flo and Meg to tell them about the party, I settled down to sleep. I felt excited about the turn life had taken. After my initial resistance, I was beginning to see what life at Porchester Park had to offer. I had been lifted out of an OK-but-ordinary world and had been transported into an extra-ordinary one. My horoscope had said that Jupiter was predominant in my chart this month, which meant expansion and that my horizons would broaden. Maybe it meant moving here.

'Bring it on, hey, Dave?' I said to the furry lump at the end of my bed. He got up, stretched, gave me a dirty look, then turned his back. Unlike me, he hadn't come around to accepting his new home just yet.

6

Settling In

By the following week, I'd got into a regular routine. Up early, go to the spa and swim for forty minutes, breakfast with Dad and Charlie, then catch the bus to school. Swimming in the pool was like going on holiday every morning and if I could practise daily, I would be well ready for the inter-school championship in December. Poppy let me use all the facilities and it was really luxurious in there, especially as I had the place to myself. The Olympic-sized pool was the perfect temperature and so pretty with its blue-and-turquoise mosaic at the bottom and the stunning painting of Neptune and his mermaids on the vaulted ceiling above, which I only saw when I turned to do backstroke.

After my swim, it was into the shower area with its enormous fluffy white towels and gorgeous Jo Malone products. I felt like a princess by the time I'd finished.

On the way back to the staff houses, if I had time, I'd have a chat with whoever was in Reception and it seemed they were all up for a bit of friendly banter and a laugh, apart from Yoram who, for some reason, seemed to regard me with suspicion and looked like he might kill me if I stepped out of line. Didier showed me his watch, which told the time in loads of different countries (though I couldn't quite see the point of that, seeing as we were in England), and Sita usually asked me how I was, what I was up to and how school was going. I soon told her about Tom and the up-and-coming fundraiser and we discussed possible outfits. Grace wasn't as friendly and barely glanced up at me from her computer screen or telephone. It always smelt divine in Reception from the enormous candle that was burnt in there daily. Sita told me that the fragrance was pomegranate noir and, like the products in the spa, was from Jo Malone. I wanted to get a candle for our house but when I looked them up online one evening when Aunt Maddie was over, I saw that a single big candle cost over two hundred pounds. Aunt Maddie had been outraged. 'Some people have money to burn. Literally!' Mum wouldn't have balked. She'd have bought one of the smaller ones which were more affordable. She loved beautiful scents and always said that you get what you pay for.

After we'd settled in, Charlie and I finally got to see

some of the apartments that had been done. Dad kept his promise and showed us three of them when he had a bit of time one evening after supper.

The first belonged to Mr and Mrs Gerard. Or Monsieur et Madame. Sieve ooh plait and ooh la la. They were Frenchies. He was an international art dealer and his apartment was like walking into an elegant, airy art gallery. They had one of the penthouses, and everywhere you looked were fabulous paintings, friezes, sculptures and artefacts.

'Lots of old stuff,' I said as I looked at an enormous painting in an ornate gold frame on the wall, then at two life-size gold statues of fat Arabian men in turbans.

'Antiques,' Dad said. 'Italian, I think.'

'Good for hanging your coat on,' I commented as I looked at one of the statues' outstretched hands.

Dad opened a door off the hallway. I peeked inside to see a dark office area with floor-to-ceiling bookshelves which were already stuffed with art books and magazines.

'Monsieur Gerard had part of a sixteenth-century French chateau shipped over for his office,' said Dad. 'Look at the mother-of-pearl inlay at the top of those shelves.'

'Wonder where her father is,' I said.

'Father?' asked Dad.

'Father of Pearl. Joke, Dad.'

In the living room, over a ginormous marble fireplace

(also from Chateau Ooh La La), was a carved mirror with gilt griffins at the top and delicate bowers of roses cascading down around the sides. I liked the look Monsieur Gerard had created: very stately home with heavy brocade and velvet curtains in reds and golds, a humungous bronze chandelier that was almost as big as me and the big squashy red sofas covered with tapestry cushions. Très posh indeedie doodie. In tall glass cabinets in the corners of the room, various masks and smaller sculptures were displayed.

'Bit scary looking,' I said as I looked at one figure with a long face and extended belly.

'Colombian,' said Dad.

'That one's had too much of their coffee, by the looks of it,' I commented as I pointed at the statue with the bloated stomach.

'Worth a fortune, each one of them,' said Dad. 'Apparently Monsieur Gerard lends parts of his collection out to museums from time to time.'

'Maybe he'd lend me the mirror with the griffins and the roses on. I'd like that,' I said as we trooped upstairs after Dad. 'We can do swapsies and he can borrow the lamp I got from Ikea this summer.'

'Yeah right,' said Dad. 'I'm sure he'd be very open to that.'

'The Chinese room?' I said as we went into a room with dark red fabric on the walls.

'Correct,' said Dad. There was a black cabinet with delicate figures and flowers painted on it, above which hung a six-foot-high portrait of two fat Chinese men.

'Maybe this is where he eats his Peking duck and noodle takeaway,' said Charlie.

'Doubt it,' said Dad. 'They have to keep these rooms at exactly the right temperature, so moisture from hot food would damage the artworks.'

'Can you imagine?' I said. 'A room for whatever food you planned on eating. An Italian room for pizza . . .'

'A French one for French fries . . .' said Charlie.

Dad rolled his eyes and led us through to a bathroom. Even that was like walking back in time, with an ancient-looking mirror filling a wall on one side and a bath with gold claw-legs standing in the centre of the room.

'Don't see the point of a mirror that you can't see yourself in,' I said. 'The glass is all foggy.'

'It's probably hundreds of years old,' said Dad. 'Imagine all the people who have looked at their reflection in it.'

'I bet they all said, "C'est un crap mirror, needs un good polish, ah oui",' I replied, in my best French accent.

'You are surrounded by works of art and history. Don't you like it?' said Dad.

'Yes. Course I do. I *do*. Way stylish. A bit like Gran's house in fact – cluttered with artefacts on every surface.'

'Yes, but unlike the junk at Gran's,' said Dad as we went back out into the hall, 'the "nick-nacks" in this apartment are worth a bomb – like the frieze in the main hall – worth at least five million. And look at the paintings stacked over there.'

'I know this print,' I said as I checked out one leaning against the wall. 'It's by Picasso.'

'And that one's a Monet,' said Charlie as he noticed another. 'I remember from art history.'

'They're not prints,' said Dad. 'They're originals.'

'As in the real thing?' asked Charlie.

Dad nodded.

'*Cool*,' I said. I wished Pia could see them.

Dad indicated a stack of other paintings lined up, waiting to be hung. 'Monsieur Gerard is one of the biggest collectors in the world. Picasso, Monet, Manet, Van Gogh, Degas. He has paintings by them all, plus a lot of modern work which I'm afraid I don't recognise but which I'm told is very collectable. Some museums would kill for a piece of this. One of the Monets sold recently for eighty million. These paintings are *all* worth many millions, so now you can understand why our security is so important.'

'Awesome,' I said. 'Think he'd like to buy one of my

sketches from art class? I have an impressive drawing of a mouldy pear. Totally original. Not another like it in the world.'

Dad smiled and ruffled my hair. 'Maybe when you're older and you've made a name as the next Tracy Emin or Damien Hirst,' he said.

'I know Damien Hirst's work,' I said. 'We saw an exhibition at the Tate on a school trip. He's the guy who does dead cows and sheep in formaldehyde. I reckon I could knock a few of those out. Totally gross, though. I know Tracy Emin's work too. She's the one who put her unmade bed on display and said it was a work of art. Easy peasy, lemon squeasy.'

Dad laughed. 'I think maybe it's a good job that you *don't* want to go into the art world, Jess.'

'I might change my mind now that I've seen Monsieur Gerard's pad. I like his style – and those old paintings.'

I sang a song from *Mamma Mia*, as Dad opened the door, and danced my way along the corridor. Charlie soon joined in, 'Money, money, money, must be funny . . . in the rich man's world . . .'

I could see that our messing about made Dad uncomfortable and I knew that there were tiny cameras discreetly placed here and there, so we didn't keep it up for long.

*

Apartment number four on the second floor had stayed with the modern look, but added a ton of marble: sand-coloured marble tiles gleamed on the walls, cream marble tiles on the floor, grey and black marble in the bathroom.

'I suppose they're going for the temple look,' I said, when I saw they had added a couple of marble pillars in the hallway too. I didn't like this one. It was posh-looking but felt cold – and not just because the heating wasn't on yet. I couldn't imagine kicking off my shoes and chilling out here. It would be like living in a hotel lobby.

To the left of the main living area was a cinema room with tiger-skin rugs, tan leather chairs, a TV screen almost as big as the wall and two life-size tiger statues on either side.

'Tack city,' I said.

Dad raised an eyebrow. 'Don't hold back on telling us what you think, Jess,' he said. As the hall opened out, there was one lovely feature and that was the circular floor, which had an enormous gold spiral pattern on it, in shades of gold. Dad told us that it had been done with real gold leaf.

'They must be bonkers,' I said. 'People are going to walk on that!' On the walls were six-foot-high paintings showing the silhouettes of sky scrapers, again done in shades of gold. It looked OK, but not to my taste.

*

73

I liked the third apartment best. It was a penthouse suite, up on the top floor. They had kept the minimal modern base but repainted in a soft off-white colour that added a touch of warmth, and they'd replaced the marble floors with some kind of light wood. In the living area, they had an arrangement of huge cream sofas that I could just see myself lounging about on, whilst looking out through the wall-to-wall glass windows onto the park beyond. Around the rooms were beautiful life-size wooden carvings. Dad said that they were Balinese. Bali-whatever, they were impressive. On a coffee table in front of the fireplace were some big art books, glossy magazines and, leaning against it, some large paintings bound up in bubble wrap, waiting to be hung. I could see through the wrap that they were abstract paintings and would bring a touch of colour to the apartment. Here and there were scented candles in glass jars and, though they hadn't been lit, their scent permeated the air, maybe jasmine, maybe sandalwood.

'I like this one best,' I said. 'It looks elegant but feels comfortable. Who's going to live here?'

'The Lewis family,' said Dad.

'Excellent,' I said. I was glad that I liked their apartment the best because I had every intention of becoming friends with them, which meant that hopefully I would be spending a lot of time up here!

I thought of our boring staff house and sighed. I'd been excited about making it nice, but having seen these amazing apartments, I felt deflated. There was no way that our house would ever look as good as these – and though I had Pia's lovely scented candle, there wasn't much else even remotely similar between the upstairs posh flats and our backstairs home.

I just hoped that I'd get to spend more time this side of the apartment block . . .

Dad left Charlie and me at the lift and headed back to his office. As we crossed the Reception area, we saw the boy from the house next door to ours lounging on one of the sofas by the right of the Reception desk, across from Didier and Yoram who were busy taking everything in: who was around; who was talking to who.

Clearly we were OK, so Yoram went back to reading his paper.

'Welcome,' said the boy on the sofa.

''Scuse me?' I said.

The boy stretched his arms behind his neck and leant back. He had a nice face with deep brown eyes and a full smiley mouth. He indicated the area with his chin. 'Welcome to my apartment block,' he said.

I laughed. 'Yeah, right.'

'And you are?'

'Charlie. And sister, Jess,' said Chaz.

'Sister Jess? Oh, a nun,' said the boy. 'In plain clothes.'

'No, dope head. I'm not a nun. I'm Charlie's sister – as in related, not as in holy holy.'

The boy grinned. 'I knew that.'

'I knew that you knew that,' I fired back.

'I knew that you knew that I knew that,' he said.

'Bit of a know-all, then, aren't you?' I said. It's a curious thing that when I don't fancy a boy, I can chat away quite happily. It's only when I really like someone that I act like an idiot and talk like I have no brain.

The boy laughed. 'I'm Henry. Son of Trevor. Dad will be looking after the bike shed.'

'Bike shed?' I asked.

'Transport,' said Henry.

'Hardly bikes,' said Charlie. 'I've been down there. Those cars are awesome. Ferraris, Mercedes, Maclarens . . .'

'Yeah, and the usual bunch of Rolls-Royces of course. To be expected,' said Henry.

'Ooh, a Rolls-Royce,' I said, in my best posh queen voice. 'How very common.'

The boys ignored me.

'Didier told me that there's a Bugatti Veyron coming,' said Charlie.

'What's a Bugatti Veyron?' I asked. 'Sounds like some kind of deadly insect.'

'Only the most awesome car *ever*,' Charlie replied.

'Costs a mere one point five two mill,' said Henry.

'For a *car*?' I gasped. 'What a waste. Who cares what it costs, does it go? That's what's important. Oh – and maybe the colour.'

Henry and Charlie exchanged a 'stupid girl, what does she know?' glance. I could see that they would be friends.

'I'm sure you could get one in pink,' said Charlie.

Henry laughed. 'So, is it just you two or is there another sister?' he asked.

Hah! So he *had* clocked Pia. I'd text her later to let her know. In the meantime, I wasn't going to make it easy for him. I was going to make him ask who Pia was.

'No, just us two. Son and daughter of Michael. The manager.'

'Yeah, but the other girl? I thought I saw you with someone.'

'I guess there is another one of us you might have seen near our window.'

'I thought so,' said Henry.

'Short, dark?'

Henry nodded.

'That would be my cat, Dave.'

'Dave?'

'Dave. So, Henry, what do you think of the place so far?'

He shrugged. 'Not sure. Different. Not exactly homely, is it?'

I sat next to him. I could tell *we* were going to get along too, not just him and Charlie.

7

New Neighbours

'Hey, something's happening,' said Charlie as we got off our bus the following Tuesday after school. We made our way up the street towards Number 1, Porchester Park, where a crowd of photographers were gathered outside the courtyard area with a very stern-looking Didier and Yoram blocking their way. The journalists weren't put off. Cameras were flashing. One man had a small stepladder and had positioned himself so he had a view over the heads of his competitors. All of them had ginormous lenses.

'Looks like paparazzi,' I said, and we hurried closer to get a better look. Behind the doormen, I could see a black limo parked at the entrance, and one of the young porters I'd seen at the staff party was taking suitcases out of the boot. *Must be the Lewis family*, I thought. Dad had mentioned that they were due to arrive today. To get my photo taken with the car or maybe even with one of them in the background would

. My cred as someone to know would become
. at school.

impsed Mrs Lewis get out of the back of the limo
and hurry into Reception. I recognised her from the
magazine I'd seen at Pia's house. She had a grey trouser
suit and dark glasses on, and looked very glamorous. A
tall man got out after her and the photographers went
crazy. It was Jefferson Lewis. He turned briefly to look
at them as their cameras flashed. He looked every inch
the screen idol, tall, dark, handsome and, from what I
could see, impeccably dressed all in black.

I managed to catch Yoram's eye. 'Can we get
through?' I asked.

Twenty pairs of eyes turned to see who had spoken.

'Who's that?' asked a short fat man.

'Go round the back, Jess, and you, Charlie,' Yoram
called. 'Use the side entrance.'

'Who are they?' asked a slim blonde woman.

'Nobody,' said Yoram.

'Nobody as in you're putting us off, or nobody as in
nobody?' demanded the short fat man.

'Nobody. Staff kids,' said Yoram, and he jerked his
chin in our direction. 'You two, hop it. Now.
Disappear.'

'Is that Jefferson Lewis?' I asked one of the photographers.

'And his family,' he replied as two tall teenagers, a

boy and a girl, were ushered inside after Mr and Mrs Lewis.

They must be Alisha and Jerome Lewis, I thought, but I couldn't see them properly through the crowd. I really wanted to stay and see what was happening, but Yoram's tone had suggested that wouldn't be a good idea, so, reluctantly, Charlie and I sloped off around to the side entrance.

'Nobody, huh?' I said. 'Cheek.'

Charlie shrugged. 'Some day we'll show them, eh?'

More residents were due to arrive the next day. I managed to slip down for my swim as usual in the morning and then had a quick nose around before school. It was just as it had been, apart from the fact that everyone who worked there was now wearing a smart suit, Yoram no longer had his nose in a newspaper and there were three tall flower arrangements on a long glass table that hadn't been there before. White orchids with green stems, maybe bamboo. Classy.

When I got back that evening, it was the same: still no sign that anything had changed or that the Lewis family had arrived the day before. Even the paparazzi had moved on. Dad said that everyone's luggage had been taken up in the lifts at the back of the building so that other residents wouldn't be disturbed and it was part of his job to keep the lobby an oasis of calm.

He seemed madly busy, though, and had organised a lady called Sheila to do our supper. She was a big smiley woman with short dark hair, an enormous chest, and a South African accent: she said yah instead of yes. I got the feeling we'd be seeing a lot of her when she asked what we liked to eat and what our favourite snacks were, then had a rummage around in the fridge and cupboards before making a shopping list of groceries.

'Even though it all looks the same, *something* has changed around here,' I said to Charlie after a supper of macaroni cheese, which Henry had joined us for. 'It's like everyone is on high alert, like they're being watched.'

'It's called working,' said Charlie.

'Will there be a welcome party when a few more of them have arrived?' I asked Dad when he popped back to pick up his BlackBerry. 'Like the one for the staff?'

Henry shook his head. 'These people don't come to meet their neighbours. They buy into a place like this for privacy.'

'Exactly,' said Dad.

'I bet their teenagers would like to meet other people their own age, though,' I said.

'Maybe,' said Dad. 'But that's up to the family, not us. OK, gotta go. Don't stay up too late.'

I felt disappointed. I'd been looking forward to

meeting Alisha and Jerome Lewis and I knew that Pia was waiting to hear all about them too.

On Friday, I got up to go for my swim as usual.

'Sorry, Jess, but you can't come in here any more,' said Poppy, when I turned up at the spa.

'I can't? Why not?' I asked.

'Mr Knight was here yesterday. He said that staff aren't allowed to use the facilities once the residents have moved in.'

I'd heard about Mr Knight. He was the owner of the complex. He was American and lived in New York. Apparently he had a similar apartment block over there in Manhattan.

'Not even me? Nobody has been using the pool this week. I've been the only one in it.'

Poppy looked harassed as the phone rang. 'Sorry, sweet pea, not even you. And I have to go – people already want treatments and I have to see who's available to do them.' She picked up the phone. Conversation over.

I was about to leave when I sensed someone standing behind me. I turned and saw a pretty dark girl in a silky turquoise top and jeans. I recognised her from her photos. Alisha Lewis.

I gave her my best smile and was about to say hi when she walked straight past me like I was invisible.

I wanted to make a comment to Poppy about it, but she was still busy on the phone. *Weird*, I thought. *What was that about?*

I made my way out of the spa and over to the Reception area for a chat with Didier. I wanted to ask him if he had met any of the new neighbours and what they were like.

'Hey, Didier, how's it going?' I said.

Didier glanced around him. 'Can't talk now, I'm working.'

'No, you're not. You're just standing there. No-one's around.'

'Not now, but they could arrive any minute.'

'You talked to me last week.'

'Place was empty then,' he said. 'Now off you go, there's a good girl.'

Place wasn't *empty*, I thought. *I was here and Charlie was here and the rest of the staff were here. Don't we count as people?* I felt upset. Hurt. Particularly by the way Alisha had snubbed me, but also because it seemed like no-one had time for me any more. Not even Sita said hi. There was no doubt about it. The atmosphere in the block had changed and I didn't like it one little bit.

Dad came through and handed Grace some papers, then turned to me.

'Hey, Jess, what are you doing here? Isn't it time for school?'

'I was going to swim but I've been told that I can't. Can you tell Poppy? I mean, you *are* the boss.'

'No, Mr Knight is the boss. I'm sorry, Jess, but it's not allowed. I meant to tell you last night but you were in bed when I got in. In fact, you shouldn't even really be here from now on, so make yourself scarce, there's a good girl, and I'll catch you later.' His mobile rang and he moved away to answer it while indicating with his left hand that I should go through the door into the staff area. He told whoever was on the phone that he'd call back in a moment, then turned to me, 'And Jess, can you tell Charlie that you both must use the side entrance from now on. You know the combination for the lock, yes? Memorised it?'

I nodded. 'Five five three zero eight four.'

'Good, and make sure you don't tell anyone.'

'Too late, I put it on Facebook,' I said, then added, '*Joke*, Dad,' when I saw how worried he looked.

'Mr Hall,' called Grace from Reception.

'Coming,' he said. 'See you after school, Jess, have a good day.'

I looked around. *So this is how it's going to be*, I thought as I watched everyone bustle around. *Good girl. Good girl. Now get lost.* Last week, I'd thought we could all be friends, but actually they'd just been like actors, waiting in the wings, sharing a laugh. Now the play had started, they were all on stage, acting their allotted roles, and no longer having time to banter with the likes of me. I felt left out. *What's my part?* I wondered. *In fact, do I even have one? Do I belong here at all?*

Later that night, Dad came up to my room. He looked tired as he sat on the end of the bed.

'Good day?' he asked.

'Not really,' I said.

He didn't appear to be listening, as he suddenly blurted out: 'Jess, I've got some bad news for you, I'm afraid. It's about Dave.'

My stomach immediately knotted. 'What about him? He's OK, isn't he?' I was sure he was. I'd seen him only an hour ago by the door, which is where he liked to position himself now, probably in the hope that he could escape the moment somebody opened it. *Please God, don't let him have got out and got lost*, I thought.

'Yes, he's fine. I'm afraid, well . . . The thing is, he can't stay. I'm really sorry but I don't make the rules. Dave got out yesterday while you were at school. Didier caught him and brought him back. I don't know how but he managed to get into the Reception area just as Mr Knight was arriving. Most unfortunate timing. Of course he asked who the cat belonged to and Yoram told him.' I scowled at that. I *knew* he had it in for me.

'He had to, Jess,' said Dad. 'It's his business to know everyone who comes through the doors, human or animal. Mr Knight wasn't happy and said that staff are here to provide service to the residents at all times – no distractions. So no pets.'

'But he's *my* pet and I'm not staff.'

'I know, love, but *I* am.'

Normally I would have made a joke about Dad not being my pet, but I didn't feel like it. 'But you don't understand. I *need* Dave. After Pia and Charlie, he's my best friend.' I felt a lump come to my throat. I couldn't imagine life without Dave. I'd had him since I was five and he'd been there to cuddle all through the good and bad times: when Mum was ill, he had seemed to sense when I was in need and would come and sit with me and put a paw up to my cheek like he understood. So no Dave? It just wasn't an option.

'I'm sorry, Jess. I'm afraid I have to insist. I want you to speak to your gran and see if she'll take him back.' He reached over to take my hand but I snatched it back under the cover.

'Maybe she'll take me back too,' I snapped.

Dad sighed. 'You never know, Jess. Dave may even be happier there.'

'No. He likes it with me. I *hate* Mr Knight. He's the meanest man in the world,' I said, even though I knew that Dave hadn't really settled here in the past few weeks. But it took time for a cat to adjust. When we first moved to Gran's after Mum's death, Dave hadn't liked it there either, but he'd soon got used to it – and he would get used to it here too, if he was just given the chance.

'I know it may seem that way, what with this and not being able to use the pool, either.'

Dad mentioning the pool made me suddenly remember that I had a meeting with the school swimming team at lunchtime the next day and that I had left my things in the spa. I got up from my bed.

'I have to go and get my swimming things, Dad. Don't worry. I'm not going to swim.'

'Do you want me to get them for you?'

I shook my head as I went out of the room. I was feeling stubborn. I didn't want Dad to do anything for me.

I felt numb as I walked down the corridor towards Reception. I had to think of a way to keep Dave. I'd beg. I'd do anything. I stood where I'd been shown so that the camera could scan my iris. I wondered if it could see rage or pain or emotion in the eye. *Probably not*, I thought, as the door opened to let me through, *it's cold and clinical just like everything and everyone else in this heartless place*.

As I got to the spa, Alisha was coming out with wet hair. I decided that I wasn't going to waste my time smiling at her again, but she looked straight at me. 'Hey,' she said.

Maybe I should give her a second chance, I thought, so I turned and smiled.

'I don't think you're supposed to be here,' she continued. 'This morning, I heard the woman at the desk saying no staff.'

'Swimming things,' I mumbled. 'Left earlier.' I pushed past her, got my things then stomped back to the staff house. I ran upstairs to call Pia, then put down the phone. What would she think? Serves me right, maybe? I so regretted having lorded it over her and everyone at school. How great it was going to be living at the new block. How my life was going up a gear and I'd be mixing with new, glamorous people. What a joke. It was completely the opposite. *This complex isn't my home, it's their home,* I thought. *I used to be Jess Hall and now who am I? Daughter of staff. Nobody. Not allowed in. Not allowed to swim in case I pollute the perfumed water. Not even allowed my cat, all because some stranger I don't even know says so. It is soooo not fair.*

I lay on my bed and the tears I had been holding back burst through. I began to sob. No Mum. No Gran. No Dave. Nobody. Life was getting worse and worse. Moments later, Dave appeared at the end of the bed. This time he didn't turn his back. He climbed onto my chest and nuzzled in.

'You and me, pal,' I said through my sobs. 'Hardly two weeks here and already, I hate Number 1, pathetic Porchester poxy Park. We both need to escape as fast as possible.'

8

Breaking the Rules

Charlie stared at the rain out of the bus window as we headed to school the next morning. He hadn't said much after I'd told him about the incident with Alisha the previous evening and that I wanted to go back and live with Gran.

'I understand, Jess,' he said, when he finally turned back to me, 'I really do. That was hard with Alisha and way harsh about Dave. I know the move has been tough on you but . . . what about me? I can't leave Dad, not now, and I don't want to go back to sleeping on the pull-out sofa at Gran's. I can't tell you how nice it is to have my own room and space again. I wouldn't go back to Gran's anyway, though, because I can see that it means a lot to Dad to have us with him.'

'Are you kidding? He hardly speaks to us these days, except to say, "Be a good girl, you shouldn't be here, make yourself scarce."'

'Yeah, well, it's make-or-break time for him. Put yourself in his shoes. He's got a new job and he has to prove he's up to it. It's a lot of responsibility and the people moving in have high standards. Way high. He can't blow it. I'm sure he'll make time for us later, when everything's up and running.'

'I guess,' I said. Dad had seemed so stressed the last few weeks, and tired. I suppose I hadn't been looking at it from his point of view. The situation was new for him too and I hadn't thought to ask how he felt.

'Listen, Jess, I'm asking you, for me. We still see Gran on a Sunday. Don't go back permanently. I don't want to be on my own.'

Charlie looked so earnest and I realised I hadn't considered *his* feelings, either. I turned to look out of the window. 'I wish Mum was still here,' I said.

'Me too,' said Charlie, in a quiet voice. 'Every day. That's why it's important we stick together. You can't run out on me now.'

I felt tears threatening. It all felt so unfair. Why did Mum have to die and leave us? An image of Charlie's face on the day of her funeral flashed into my head. He'd looked so pale, so shell-shocked. He'd been dressed in a smart jacket that Dad had got him, a shirt and tie too, not his style at all. Everything about that day had seemed wrong. Charlie shouldn't have been dressed like that. Mum shouldn't have died. Going to her funeral was not something I'd expected to happen. Ever. Mum had always been there. Solid and dependable. Getting me up in the morning. Nagging me to bed at night. Putting food in the fridge, soap, toothpaste and loo paper in the bathroom. A million small things I'd taken for granted until she wasn't there. But the funeral *had* happened. A wet day not unlike today. Unreal but final. I'd felt so confused, having thoughts that were all wrong, thoughts I could never tell anyone, not even Pia or Charlie, because I was ashamed of them and they meant that I was the worst person in the world. Part of me couldn't take it in and imagined I'd wake up and it would all have been a bad dream, a nightmare, and Mum's face would reappear around my door the next day and say, 'Phew, glad that weird episode is over, now let's get on with the rest of our lives.' But she never did. She didn't come back. She was gone forever and slowly all trace of her loving care disappeared: the little treats in the biscuit tin for Chaz and me that only she knew to buy; our favourite breakfast cereal – Shreddies for Chaz, Alpen for me; my favourite Fruits of the Forest shampoo; fizzy drinks, crisps and a DVD on a Friday night. Little things that added up to having a real-life mum watching out for us. All gone.

I thought about Charlie on his own. How could I have thought about going back to Gran's and leaving him, even for a moment? No. I couldn't do it to him.

'All the tears and sadness in the world can't bring her back,' he said as if picking up on my thoughts. 'She's gone. We're still here. We have to adapt, adjust and be positive. It's a new chapter and we have to help each other.'

'I won't leave you,' I said.

He didn't say anything for a while. 'Nor me you,' he said at last. 'Us against the world, eh? At least we have our mates and a life outside Porchester Park where we can be ourselves.'

Outside the school gates, a small crowd of pupils were gathered.

Sophie James pointed as me and Charlie got off the bus.

'There they are!' she said, and everyone turned to look at us.

'What's going on?' asked Charlie.

'No idea,' I said and looked behind us to see if they meant someone else.

'Hey, can I take a photo for the school mag?' asked Chrissie Alberg as we reached the gates.

'A photo? Of me? Why?' I asked.

Chrissie pulled out a paper and showed me a page. A-LISTERS MOVE INTO KNIGHTSBRIDGE APARTMENT BLOCK, said the headline, and there was a photo of the Lewis family with a smaller shot underneath of the entrance at Number 1, Porchester Park.

'That's where you live, isn't it?' asked Sarah Marcuson from the Sixth Form.

'Yeah,' said Charlie. 'So what?'

'What's it like living with stars?' asked a wide-eyed girl from Year Eight.

Charlie glanced at me. He had a twinkle in his eye. 'Words can never describe it,' he said.

I laughed. *Too right*, I thought. *Words can't describe how totally cold and friendless the place is.*

'Living the dream,' I said. 'We're living the dream.' What I didn't add was that it was a bad dream.

'I am *so* jealous,' said the wide-eyed girl.

Meg and Flo arrived, linked arms with me, and pulled me away.

'And we're the private bodyguards,' Flo called over her shoulder. 'Mess with us and you're . . . um . . . messy.'

I laughed.

'Mates stick together,' said Meg. 'We have to look after you now that you're in with the in-crowd.' She did a spontaneous kung fu move. 'I could karate-chop them out the way.'

'Yeah right,' I said. Meg might do karate after school but she was still tiny and not exactly bodyguard material.

'And are you OK, Charlie?' asked Flo, with a coy glance in his direction. She'd fancied him since junior school although he was totally oblivious to the fact.

'Oh, tippety-top, aren't we, Jess?' replied Charlie.

'If you say so,' I said.

Just inside the gates, I spotted Tom Robertson with Josh and Roy. They were watching us with interest. I stared straight at Tom and he didn't look away. He held my gaze and raised an eyebrow, as if to acknowledge a connection. I felt my stomach do a double flip. I didn't let on. I was going to show him that I could be Queen of Cool as well as Queen of the Zombies. I looked away like I was really bored. Oh so casual, like, whatever, Tom Robertson. *Let them believe that everything's hunky-dory*, I thought. *Charlie and I know the truth, but why shatter everyone else's illusions?*

'Hi, Charlie,' said Tom as we went past. Then he looked at me. 'See you've got your jacket on the right way around this time.'

Charlie nodded back at Tom, then leant over and whispered, 'Yesterday a nobody, today a somebody.'

Yeah. If only they knew, I thought, as we walked into school while Sophie's camera flashed and the rest of the crowd followed us as if we were the celebrities and they were paparazzi. I didn't want to be a somebody. Not this way – by association with people who had a low opinion of me. It felt fake. I wanted to be able to walk into school and go through the day as I always had done. One of the gang. Just me. Invisible most of the time. As I passed Tom, I could feel that he was still watching me, but I didn't even glance at him.

Later, in class, Mrs Rushton took the register. She peered over her glasses when she got to my name.

'And Jess Hall,' she said. 'I believe you've moved up to the big time and are living with celebrities.'

'Not really, Miss,' I said. 'Same ol'.'

Mrs Rushton regarded me for a moment. 'Well, just so that you don't let it go to your head, you can start the reading today. Turn to page fourteen of *The Lord of the Flies* and stand up so everyone can hear.'

So much for wanting to be invisible. I hated reading out loud. Sometimes being a nobody had its benefits.

After school, I went to the local baths to get my swimming practice in. I couldn't help but compare things there to the luxury pool back at Porchester Park. The floors had bits of hair and dust in the corners and needed cleaning after a day open to the public. The showers were cold and the pool was full – so I couldn't swim without being careful that I didn't bash into someone – and the smell was more chlorine than Jo Malone. Those few days had been so good in the apartments' pool and part of me wished I hadn't been there, so I couldn't compare it now. I didn't have a choice, though. If I was going to win my race at the championship in December I had to practise every day, no matter what the conditions.

When I got home from swimming, Dave was waiting by the door. I picked him up and he nuzzled my nose and purred loudly. I carried him into the kitchen and put some food out in a bowl for him.

As I watched him eat, I went to get the phone to call Gran. I'd promised Dad that I would ask her about Dave going back to her. I dialled her number then put down the phone. It didn't feel right. Never mind leaving Charlie, I couldn't leave Dave on his own at Gran's. He would miss me and he'd seemed more settled in the last few days. Charlie's words from earlier that morning echoed in my head. 'It's important we stick together.' Surely that meant Dave too? It would be cruel to abandon him. He was part of our family as well.

A few minutes later, the phone rang. I picked it up to hear Gran at the other end.

'Was that you, Jess?' she asked. 'I heard the phone ring then it cut off.'

'Oh. Yes. Me. Just checking in.'

'How are things there? I'll be over at the weekend. I thought you and I could start to plan the garden. What do you think?'

'Sounds great.'

'And how's it going?'

'Oh, we're living the dream Gran, living the dream.'

'Dream? What dream? What are you talking about?'

'I . . . oh, nothing. It's just a way of saying, yeah, everything's cool.' Part of me longed to tell her what I really felt but I knew she'd worry and be on Dad's case. I owed it to Charlie to give the new situation a bit longer.

As we chatted on, a plan began to form in my mind. After I hung up, I made a decision.

'Dave,' I said. 'It's me, you and Charlie against the world.'

Dave meowed, as if in agreement. As Dave continued with his supper, I whizzed around the house collecting his belongings: his felt cat house, the old cardi he liked to sleep on, Charlie's sock (well chewed) that he liked to play with, his toy mouse. I put them all in a carrier bag, then collected his food bowls, the sachets of cat food and crunchies from the cupboard. I found the torch that Gran had given me, unlocked the back door and took Dave's things down to the summerhouse. Once I'd cleared a bit of space, I went back to collect Dave before Sheila arrived to do our supper and before Dad or Charlie appeared.

Dave purred loudly when I stepped into the garden, probably thinking he was to be allowed out at last.

'Not just yet,' I said, as I opened the summerhouse

door and put him down inside. 'Our secret. You have to stay in here and be a good boy.' I turned around and faced the apartment block. 'So there, Mr Stinky Knight with your rules about what I can and can't do. I stay stuff them and stuff you. Why should you tell me what to do when you don't even know me? Well, I have news for you, pal, and it's that I'm keeping my cat!'

Before I could change my mind, I closed the summerhouse door. At least I would be able to go and visit Dave every day. Dad would see that Dave and his things had gone but he'd never know the truth, and Dave and I wouldn't be separated after all.

Sorted.

9

Cat-astrophe

'Wowza,' said Pia when she saw my newly-painted bedroom. 'It looks great.'

It was late Sunday morning and she'd come over to help me with some finishing touches. We'd chosen the paint colours together on Friday night from some cards with colour samples on that Dad had sent out for earlier in the week. Aunt Maddie had also come over to join us for an hour. I'd expected her to suggest that I paint my room green to go with her new interest in life but, strangely, she had been total sweetness and light and not done her prison warder act at all. She was actually quite civil for a change.

Dad had also been bending over backwards to be nice the last few days and said that he would make it up to me after I told him that Dave was now back at Gran's. I didn't like lying to him but felt I had no choice. I couldn't let Dave go, but he didn't like it in the summerhouse, I could tell. It already smelt of cat because I couldn't always get down there to change his litter tray after school, not since Sheila had started coming earlier. She was usually in the kitchen doing mine and Charlie's supper when I got back these days.

Today, my plan was to let Dave into the house so that he could roam about while Dad was out. Charlie, who didn't know about Dave, had already gone off to practise with his band mates.

Dad popped his head around the door. 'Hi, Pia. Looks nice, doesn't it?'

Pia nodded. 'The painters were fast.'

He came in and inspected the walls. 'Yes. And they did a good job.' He'd asked some of the handymen on his staff to come in on Saturday and between the four of them, they'd bought the paint and got the job done by the evening. I'd slept on the sofa downstairs while the room dried and this morning, it was ready to move back in to. The room was a pale turquoise on three walls and a deep lavender on the fourth. I'd seen the colours in a magazine and it looked bright and colourful, loads better than the bland white it had been before.

Dad saw that I had a photo of Dave already out in pride of place next to my bed. 'I really am sorry about Puss,' he said, and he genuinely did look sad.

'I . . . oh, yeah, it's so not fair,' I mumbled. I wasn't

sure how to play it: whether to act sulky like I'd obeyed him and Dave was at Gran's or whether to pretend to be OK, as if I was trying to be positive.

'Not my rules,' said Dad. 'I'd have let him stay. You do know that, don't you?'

Pia had gone bright red. 'You could get her a stuffed cat,' she said in a high, nervous voice.

Dad and I looked at her as if she was mad. She *was* mad – as if a stuffed toy could take the place of a living breathing cat.

As soon as Dad had gone, I waited five minutes then nodded to Pia.

'Right, let's go and get Dave. It's Sheila's day off and she's left us some pizza to warm up. Charlie won't be back until this evening and Dad will be gone most of the day.'

'What about your gran?' asked Pia. 'I thought she was coming over.'

'At four,' I said and checked my watch. 'It's eleven now so we have loads of time. I'll go and get him.'

I raced downstairs and out to the summerhouse where Dave almost leapt into my arms. He struggled to escape as I carried him across the garden but I couldn't risk letting him down in case he jumped up onto the fence and took off. 'You can run around in the house,' I said to him, as Pia held the kitchen door open for us. I plonked him down and we quickly shut the door.

Dave meowed as if to say, *free at last*, then took off on a major sniffathon, his nose hoovering up every smell.

'We'll just let him roam about,' I said, 'and we can carry on in my room.'

We spent the next few hours adding the finishing touches to my room. A dark turquoise duvet cover with lavender cushions, to which we added one purple cushion for a splash of deeper colour. My poster of the Drunken Popes, my favourite boy band. Photos of Chaz, Mum and me at Christmas and one of Mum wearing a crazy bathing cap with plastic flowers stuck on the side. My pale pink rug on the floor. My fave books on the bookshelf under the window. A few glossy mags that Pia had brought over from her mum. The scented candle. With my familiar things around, it was beginning to feel more like home.

'Looks fanbloomingtastic,' said Pia, when we had finished and flopped down on the bed. 'Très chic.'

'Where's Dave?' I said, suddenly realising that I hadn't seen him since we'd had a break for lunch over an hour ago.

'Under the bed?' Pia suggested.

I got down on my knees and had a look. No Dave. 'I'd better check no-one left a window open,' I said as sudden panic gripped me. I checked downstairs first. All the windows were shut. Then Charlie's room. Also safe.

'So where could he be?' asked Pia.

'Dad's room?' I suggested and we both went to look. A horrible smell hit us as soon as we got there.

'Oh NO!' cried Pia. She pointed to the bed where a small pile of poo and a yellow stain lay right in the middle of the duvet.

'He's pooed on the bed! Dave, where are you?' I looked around the room. Dave's head appeared from under the bed. He hopped up onto the covers and stood next to his deposit with a smug look on his face. 'Naughty cat! Why did you do that?'

Pia picked him up and cuddled him. 'Don't be cross. Cats do it when they're upset and, let's face it, he has every reason to be. I remember my aunt had cats and one of them always peed on the bed whenever they had guests or builders in.'

Dave didn't look in the slightest bit upset. In fact, he looked very pleased with himself. I couldn't be cross with him, though. It couldn't have been nice for him being cooped up in the summerhouse on his own and I understood that this was his way of making his objections known. I looked at my watch. 'Oh hell, it's three o'clock. I've got an hour before Gran gets here. I have to get this cleaned up.' I raced into the bathroom and got a roll of toilet paper.

'Yuck,' I said as I wrapped up Dave's small gift to Dad, then flushed it away down the loo.

Back in Dad's room, Pia pulled the duvet cover off and then the sheets. 'Oh no, Jess. It's gone right through to the mattress.'

I looked where she was pointing. She was right. The stain had gone all the way through and, boy, it stank. I ran down the stairs to the kitchen and found the bucket under the sink, filled it with hot water then looked for all the cleaning products that I could find.

Back upstairs, Dave was still looking well smug.

'Take that look off your face, mister, you're in the doghouse,' I said.

Pia cracked up laughing.

'Not funny,' I said as I liberally sprayed cleaner on the mattress then began to scrub.

'Tis,' said Pia. 'Doghouse.'

Twenty minutes later, the room smelt of disinfectant and cleaning products. The bed, however, was soaked. There was no way I was going to get it dry before Gran came and she was bound to want to have a look around to see what we had done since her previous visit.

'Hairdryer,' suggested Pia.

'Brilliant,' I said. 'Oh, except I haven't got a hairdryer. Only hair straighteners.'

Pia cracked up again. 'Get them,' she said, when she'd stopped laughing. 'They're better than nothing.'

'Well, I'm glad *someone* is finding this so amusing,' I said.

'OK. Iron,' said Pia. I could see she was still having a hard time not laughing. I gave her a dirty look and she attempted to look serious.

'The straighteners are in my bedroom,' I said. 'You get them and plug them in.'

I raced back down the stairs and got the iron – back up the stairs, plugged it in, let it get hot then applied it to the mattress, as Pia got busy with the duvet cover and the hair straighteners. A little of the dampness disappeared on the bed but there was still a great big wet patch.

'And the cover sheet,' Pia reminded me as she looked at it draped over a chair.

'Oh God, Dad is going to kill me,' I said. 'What am I going to say?'

Pia shrugged. 'Um, a pipe burst?'

I looked around. There were no pipes anywhere to be seen. I had an idea.

'Pia, you're my friend, yeah?'

'Er . . . yeah?'

'You once said that you'd do anything for me . . .'

'Um . . . yeah...'

'We *could* say that you came in here and spilt some water.'

'Right in the middle of the bed? Why would I be in here? And why all the disinfectant if it was only water?'

'Yes, good point? Um, OK, maybe not, then. Maybe I could say Charlie did it. Um, spilt coffee.'

'But your dad knows Charlie is out all day.'

'OK, OK, I could say I did it, then. My room still smelt of paint and so I came in here with a cup of coffee and it spilt.'

'Perfect,' said Pia. 'He can't be mad about that.'

'In the meantime, we have to get everything immaculate,' I said. I picked up the iron in one hand and the hair straighteners in the other and held them aloft as if they were weapons. 'Captain Muckremover here and his trusty assistant. We go where most people fear to tread.'

Pia laughed and picked up a hairbrush and a bottle of aftershave from the cabinet by the bed. She sprayed a little of the scent into the room.

I started to do a rap dance. 'Me and Pia, we are the crew, don't call us, we'll call you.'

Pia joined in, singing her own verse, 'Me and Jess, we are the crew, we fight the muck, remove cat poo.'

That set us off laughing and we couldn't stop. The whole situation seemed suddenly hilarious. We tried to do a bit more drying but neither of us could focus and kept cracking up. The sight of Pia on the floor with her bum in the air desperately trying to dry my dad's bed cover with my hair straighteners struck me as the funniest thing I'd ever seen. When Dave leapt up onto the bed and looked for a moment like he was going to do it again, Pia fell over, crying tears of laughter. At that moment, we heard a noise down below, then footsteps coming up the stairs.

'Oh God, who's that?' I gasped. Pia and I looked at each other and the wet sheets and duvet and Dave sitting there proud as anything on the bed.

'Quick, under the bed,' I said. 'It might be Charlie come back for something.'

We grabbed Dave and dived under the bed just as the door opened.

It wasn't Charlie. It was Dad.

Oops.

10

Doghouse

I am in the doghouse. Or in the shitola – the cat shitola, as Pia said, before she made a quick exit leaving
me to face Dad and Gran, who turned up ten minutes
later. Pia's shoulders were still shaking with laughter as
she left. Dad told me to wait upstairs while he talked to
Gran, and from an upstairs window, I watched Pia make
her way towards the staff gate. Henry was just coming
in. He stopped and said something to her. She'd be well
pleased that she'd got to talk to him. I watched them
chat for a few minutes, then she clearly told him what
had happened because I saw him crack up, then glance
over at the house. Pia said something else and he
cracked up again. I am going to kill her next time I see
her.

I could still hear Dad and Gran's voices below, so I
went and waited on the landing to listen in as they
argued about how I should be punished. I could tell that
Dad was really mad.

'Losing her cat is enough, Michael,' I heard Gran say.

'Yes, but she crossed the line,' I heard Dad reply. 'I have to set boundaries.'

I stroked Dave who was on my knee. 'Looks like you might have to go after all, pal,' I said as I buried my face in his fur.

Five minutes later, Dad called me down.

Gran came over and put her arm around me, while Dad hovered anxiously.

'I've decided that you're to be grounded, Jess,' he said.

'Grounded?'

Dad nodded. 'You go to school, then you come straight back. For a week.'

'A *week*? But Dad, I have to practise my swimming, you know how important the competition at the end of term is! Either before school or after – and Friday night is the fundraiser. I can't miss that. I *can't*. Only a few of us have been invited to represent the school.'

Gran glanced at Dad.

Dad shook his head. 'You'll have to miss the fundraiser. This is what happens when you overstep the mark. You miss out on things. I'm sorry, Jess, but that's my final word.'

'*Mum* would have let me go. She'd have been proud of me. Only fifty people have been selected from the whole *school*,' I said. I could tell my response had hit the mark because Dad looked pained. He glanced at Gran, who slightly tilted her head as if to say, *Get out of this one, matey.*

'No, Jess. I'm sure your mother would have agreed with me. You were out of order, not to mention what that poor cat must have been going through in the summerhouse. I thought you were an animal lover. You know cats need space to roam.'

His last remark got me. I was going to cry. I hadn't liked having to lock Dave up, not one bit. 'I'm glad he pooed on your bed,' I blurted. 'You asked for it.'

'Now, Jess, go to your room before either of us says any more. I think we all need to cool down.' He glanced at his watch and shuffled on his feet. 'I have to go.' He looked at Gran. 'You're going to be here for a bit, aren't you?'

Gran nodded and looked at me sympathetically but I didn't want anyone to be kind or understanding. I felt like having a major three-year-old type tantrum.

'I hate you,' I said to Dad. I gathered Dave into my arms, ran up the stairs into my room and slammed the door. 'ArghARGHHHHHHHHH!'

Dave looked at me with concern as I lay on my bed. *No-one understands*, I thought. *Life is so unfair and I hate everyone. Apart from Dave, and now he's going to be taken away.* The tears came flooding forward and I burst into angry, frustrated sobs.

Ten minutes later, there was a knock at the door. I didn't answer. I heard the door open and Gran came in with a tray with two mugs and a plate of toast and Marmite on it. She set it down on the bookshelf, then sat on the end of the bed.

I still didn't say anything.

'It's looking nice in here,' she said as she looked around, and she put her hand on my foot. I sat up, squiggled over to her and buried my head in her lap. She stroked my hair as I cried my eyes out.

When there were no more tears, Gran made me eat some toast and coaxed me downstairs, where she made more tea in the kitchen.

'You do know Dave has to come with me, don't you?' she asked.

I nodded. 'I knew he wasn't happy in the summer-house and . . . and . . .' I felt myself starting to sob again, 'I do want what's best for him.'

'I know, love,' said Gran.

'I'm so used to him sleeping on the end of the bed. We've never been apart. Ever.'

'I know how hard it is for you to let him go, but he knows my house, he's safe in the garden and you can come and visit whenever you want, every day if you want.'

'When I'm allowed out again,' I said.

'Yes. That. Listen, Jess, you be a really good girl this

week and you never know, your dad might soften in time for that fundraiser, at least.'

I shrugged. I doubted it. I'd seen the look on his face when I said that I hated him.

'I'll apologise,' I said. 'I don't really hate him. At least not *all* of the time.'

Gran smiled. 'I know. You're a good girl, Jess. And a brave one.'

I felt my eyes fill up with tears again. 'Don't be nice to me, Gran. I'm not a nice girl.'

Gran laughed. 'OK. You're a bad *bad* girl, then. Just awful.'

I laughed. Gran reached over and put her hand over mine and I wondered whether to tell her about my secret from the day of Mum's funeral. I was longing to confide in someone, but somehow I just couldn't. Gran loved me and I wouldn't be able to bear it if she thought badly of me. 'Give it time here, Jess,' she said. 'The first few weeks are always the worst in a new situation. Now, tell me everything. How it's really been. The truth.'

I told her exactly how it had been since we'd moved and she listened without interrupting. After I'd got it all out, she gave me a big hug then we went into the garden and talked about what we could plant and what she'd bring over. I knew she meant well but I couldn't summon much enthusiasm because I knew what was coming next and all too soon, it was time for her and Dave to go. We looked out Dave's cat basket and he got into it happily as if he knew the plan and understood.

'Neither of us belong here,' I said to the black-and-white furry face looking out at me. 'At least you get to escape.'

Dave did a silent meow by way of an answer.

After Gran had gone, I went down to the summer-house and cleared out his cat litter tray, then went back to the house. It was so quiet, the surfaces gleaming in the kitchen where Gran had cleaned, the empty rooms. I went and sat on the bottom stair where I'd held Dave only a few hours earlier and felt like my heart was going to break.

11

Grounded

Diary of a prisoner:

<u>Monday</u>. School. Afterwards, Meg went to her karate class, Pia went to drama and Flo was going to watch a romantic comedy with her cousin. Not fair. I had to come straight home. Homework, supper, then bed. Boring. My life sucks.

<u>Tuesday</u>. School. Tom Robertson said hi on the way out of assembly. I said hi back. Ah, my scintillating love life. Not. Home. Saw Mrs Lewis at the front getting into a car. She stared at me. I felt like putting my hand over my face and saying, 'No photos, please,' but it might have got back to Dad and I am being Miss Goodytwoshoes this week. Gran rang. Dave is happy, she said, and I can go and visit when I'm allowed out again. I'm trying to be positive but I feel miffed with everyone. I didn't ask to come and live here so I feel cross I have to abide by the stupid rules made by Mr Horrible Knight. I feel like my swimming will be

suffering through lack of practice. I will lose my race and let the team down. I am turning into a blob already. A bitter, twisted blob. I hate my life. Bed.

<u>Wednesday</u>. School. I'm still being asked by ignorant people about living where I do. Huh. If only they knew the real story. I am locked up. My cat has been taken away. It sucks big time. I apologised to Dad at supper-time and told him I didn't really hate him. He looked very relieved. He apologised too and said that with all the people moving in, he has been rushed off his feet. I hadn't realised that more residents had arrived because I wasn't speaking to Dad for the first part of this week, but apparently the family from Saudi Arabia have moved in with their entourage and so has the art dealer man and his wife and a Russian couple and their children plus a Japanese family and one of their daughters. I haven't seen them, as I go in and out through the staff area and when I do go into the main block, Yoram always gives me such filthy looks as if to say, *Get outta here, and I mean now!* On the rare occasions I've had to go and find Dad or take a message, there always seems to be something going on – glam people swanning about, men in dark suits in dark glasses talking into their phones, limos out the front dropping people off, all busy busy, living their fabbie dabbie lives. No-one looks very friendly. Round the back at the service lift, near the tradesmen's entrance,

some days it looks like an Aladdin's cave with packages and boxes from Harrods, Fortnum & Mason's, racks of fabulous-looking clothes being wheeled into the lift, designer carrier bags, fabulous deliveries of fresh flowers, gorgeous furniture and mirrors being taken up – all sorts of stuff. I'd love to ask who it's all for, what it is, can I have a look? But I know that I can't be nosey or Yoram might try to put a hitman onto me.

I still feel bad that I haven't been able to do my swimming practice. If I am to win the junior championship, I really do have to swim every day. I tried to 'dry swim' on the floor in my room to keep my muscles active and Charlie came in and said I'd now confirmed to him that I am totally mad. Flo, Meg and Pia sent me some nice messages on Facebook. Haha. Dad doesn't realise how much time I spend on there instead of doing my homework. Bed.

Thursday. School. Mr Bennie, our swimming teacher, asked me how my practice was going. I said good because I couldn't tell him about what had happened on Sunday and why I'd been grounded. He said, 'Remember the rules, Jess – practise, practise every day.' I agreed. I made Pia, Meg and Flo laugh at lunchtime by lying on the floor in the corridor outside the library and showing them my 'dry swimming' breaststroke technique. Pia and Meg joined in while Flo looked on. She doesn't do bonkers, she's too busy being ethereal, and acting mad on the corridor floor would not be the sort of thing an elfin princess would do. Mary Johnson, a prefect in Year Eleven, told Pia, Meg and me to get up, stop being stupid and acting like frogs. I said I wasn't being a frog, I was practising my swimming. Pia did a ribbit noise. It was pretty impressive, I thought. Mary said we were juvenile and possibly insane. She may be right. I have been driven to it by circumstances. Saw Tom in the corridor outside the library. He smiled at me. He didn't get it when Pia made her ribbit noise. I pretended I didn't know her. Tom laughed. Home.

Made some choc-chip cookies for Dad and Charlie after Sheila had gone. Dad didn't hang around and had to go out to have dinner with Mr Poo Stink Bum Knight. He said he'd be back late. Henry dropped by and we watched a sci-fi film. Not really my thing – seeing people get their heads ripped off and spew green slime. Charlie and Henry loved it, though, but then boys are naturally an alien species. Bed early. Then got out of bed. I'd had an idea.

The rules for the apartment block weren't my rules. My rules were relevant to my life and were the ones decreed by Mr Bennie, the swimming coach. Practise, practise.

Which were more important? Mr Knight's or Mr Bennie's?

If I followed Mr Knight's rules, I would let the swimming team down.

If I followed Mr Bennie's, I would let Dad down. But then he had said I was grounded and couldn't leave the apartment block. The spa was in the apartment block, wasn't it? No-one would be there at this time of night. Henry had left almost half an hour ago and I'd heard Charlie clomp his way up the stairs. So . . . I stuck my head into his room. He was lying on his bed, eyes shut, with his headphones on. He didn't even open his eyes.

I went back to my room, got my swimming things, then crept downstairs, out of the house, and into the corridor that led to Reception. I stood before the iris scanner – and open sesame – the door let me in. At Reception, I could see Sita on the telephone. She waved me over.

'What are you doing here?' she asked.

'Dad asked me to collect a letter that Poppy left on her desk in the spa,' I said. It wasn't a complete lie. He had asked me to do something similar just a week ago. Sita didn't need to know details of times or dates.

The phone rang and Sita picked it up and nodded at me as if to say, *Off you go*. Didier was standing outside the front door and glanced over. I wondered if he was going to ask where I was going, but he just lifted his chin, which in chin speak is 'hi', then turned back to look outside.

I crossed Reception and went down the stairs, through the doors and into the spa area. All was quiet, as I'd expected. Nightlights on either side of the stairs and corridor softly lit the way to the pool area. Nobody was around. I checked my watch. Ten-thirty. I'd be able to do about thirty lengths and then be back in bed before Dad even noticed that I was missing. I got changed and minutes later I was in the water. It was the perfect temperature. Heaven.

I'd swum only about ten lengths when I heard voices. My heart thudded in my chest. Hells bells, who was it? I swam to the side, jumped out and ran to hide behind a large basket that was used during the day for wet towels. From my vantage point there, I willed the ripples I'd made in the pool to disappear as I saw Alisha and a boy of about seventeen step into the area. Jerome Lewis. I recognised him from his photo in the paper. Alisha looked at the water. I knew she could tell someone had been swimming because she looked around, shrugged and said something to Jerome. I waited for them to disappear into the changing room so I could make a run for it.

Oh no, I thought, just as I was about to make my move, *I've left my stuff in there. What shall I do? Run anyway while they're in there? They might not know the clothes are mine. Why would they? They might assume one of the other residents has left them. But I can't run away because I can't cross Reception in my cossie . . .*

The decision was taken out of my hands, because Jerome and Alisha reappeared moments later. They were wearing robes that they took off and hung up by the door. I shrank down, trying to make myself invisible, and to calm my breathing in case they heard me. I watched as they approached the pool. Jerome Lewis was a one hundred per cent hunky mcdunky. Tall and handsome with a well fit body. He dived in at the deep end and began to swim. He had an excellent style and smoothly cut his way through the water. Alisha soon joined him and swam too although Jerome looked like the stronger swimmer. I stayed in my place in agony because I was kneeling on my feet and they tingled with pins and needles. I didn't dare move, in case one of them saw me.

Stupid, stupid girl. I told myself. *What possessed me to come down here? And now it's getting late. What if Dad comes back? I'll be grounded for another week, month, year – the rest of eternity, probably. Oh God, my life is sooooo miserable and now I am trapped.*

After what seemed an interminable length of time, Jerome got out.

'Going for a shower,' he called to his sister. 'You gonna be long?'

'Two minutes,' said Alisha, and she looked directly at the towel basket. 'But I'm going to shower upstairs. You never know who's been using these public ones.'

121

'When did you become Miss Prissy Pants?' asked Jerome, then disappeared into the changing area.

'I'll wait for you,' Alisha called after him.

She knows I'm here, I thought and indeed, moments later, she got out of the pool, went over to the pile of clean, white towels, picked one out and dried herself off a little. When she'd finished, she sauntered towards the towel basket and dropped the wet towel in.

'I know you're there,' she said.

There was no pretending. She came around and looked right at me. I got up but almost fell over because my feet were numb. I limped out as blood rushed back into my toes, causing them to tingle even more.

'I thought you weren't supposed to be here,' she continued, without looking at me.

I stooped over and touched a mock cap like I'd done when I'd been in a play at school years ago and was playing a poor farmer. 'Oh sorry, ma'am, I beg pardon,' I said. 'I know poor peasants like me unt allowed to mix with you proper ladies like. It won't 'appen again. Oo ar.'

Alisha looked at me with surprise. My reaction clearly wasn't what she'd expected and, for a brief moment, she actually looked like she was going to laugh.

I didn't hang around to find out, though, and made as swift an exit as I could considering my tingling feet.

I wasn't going to go and get my clothes and risk bumping into Jerome in case he was as sour as his sister. I walked over to the clean towels and wrapped one around myself, trying not to show her how intimidated I was. I let myself out of the pool-room and into the spa area. Poppy was back from wherever she'd been and was sitting at her desk. She looked up.

'Jess?'

'Oh God, Poppy, sorry. Won't do it again. Sorry, sorry, please don't tell Dad.'

Poppy shrugged a shoulder. 'Have you been swimming?'

I nodded.

'Do what you like. I won't tell your dad. In fact, I don't think I'm going to be around much longer.'

I noticed she had no make-up on and looked tired. 'Why? What's happened?'

She jerked her chin towards the pool-room. 'I didn't sign up for a twenty-four-hour-a-day service. This new lot of residents have only been here a week and already I can't keep up with their demands. I can't imagine what it's going to be like when all the apartments are full. I was asleep just now. *Asleep!* I was worn out running around after all of them and then I get woken up because someone wants to use the pool. Honestly, it's almost eleven o'clock! If they want to use the pool, let them. Why do I have to be here? To pick up their used towels and make sure the lights are on? It's been the same every night this week. Don't these people sleep? I mean, I don't mind hard work but . . . no, not this. It's not for me, being somebody's slave.'

'So what will you do?'

Poppy shrugged. 'Oh, I don't know. Ask me in the morning. Sorry. Just letting off steam. I know someone has to be here. Health and safety rules and all that. Anyway, you'd better beat it before the Lewises come out.'

'You won't tell Dad, will you?'

Poppy shook her head. 'And don't you tell him I've been moaning either, will you? Just, I need my beauty sleep and I'm tired.'

'Your secret's safe with me. Hey, you haven't got a robe behind there, have you? So I can cross Reception? Oh – and an envelope?'

Poppy leant down, pulled out a white robe and handed it to me.

'Oh, and Poppy, I'm really sorry to ask but I left my stuff in the changing room. I can't go back and get it because her Royal High-and-Mightiness and her brother are in there, I—'

Poppy nodded wearily. 'I'll get your stuff. I'll take it with me when I leave and you can pop into my house and get it.'

'You're a star.'

'Aren't I just?'

I slipped the robe on and then raced back up through Reception where I waved to Sita and Didier, who were deep in conversation.

'Got it,' I said and I held up the envelope so they could see. Neither of them seemed to notice that I was in different clothes, thank God.

Five minutes later, I was back at the house. Luckily Dad wasn't home yet and the light was off in Charlie's room, so he must have gone to sleep.

Phewee, lucky escape, I thought as I crept back into bed.

12

Chaperone?

'Will you do it again?' asked Pia as we got off the bus and headed towards Porchester Park.

I shook my head. 'No way, José. I'm back in Dad's good books. Can you imagine if he found out?'

Pia linked her arm through mine. 'You'd be a prisoner forever and no-one would ever see you again. I'm so glad he's letting you come to the fundraiser.'

It was Friday evening and we were heading back to my house to get ready for the event this evening at school. I had wanted to get changed at Pia's, but she'd insisted that we go back to mine. I know why. She's hoping to bump into Henry again. It's true love. I know, because since she met him on the day of Dave's poo disaster, she's written his name in a heart over and over in the margin of her journal. I think he likes her too because every time I see him, he asks about her. Love was definitely in the air, plus, tonight at the fundraiser, I was hoping I'd get the chance to take things with Tom past smiling in the corridor stage and into major flirt mode.

We walked past the main entrance and I waved at Didier, who waved back.

'Do you always have to use the side entrance now?' asked Pia, as we made our way there.

'Until I make my first billion,' I said, 'and then I'll waltz through the front with the rest of them, looking down my nose at Princess Snotola Bogeyface, Alisha Lewis.'

Pia tightened her grip on my arm. 'Ohmigod, there they are,' she said.

I looked over and saw that a black limo had pulled up outside the main entrance. Stuart, one of the valets, appeared out of nowhere and opened the door. Mrs Lewis, Alisha and Jerome got out. I spotted Dad hovering by the door as if he wanted to talk to them, while Mrs Lewis looked straight at me and Pia.

'She's looking at us,' said Pia. 'What do we do?'

'We act normal,' I said, but part of me was panicking because Mrs Lewis said something to Alisha, they both looked at me and then went over to talk to Dad.

I am dead, I thought. *Alisha's sneaked on me to her mum and now probably wants to make a complaint about me being in the pool last night.*

I tugged on Pia's arm. 'Come on, let's go,' I said and we set off again for the side entrance, but Didier came running after us.

'Hey, Jess, your dad wants you,' he said. I turned back to see that everyone was looking at me: Dad, Mrs Lewis, Alisha and Jerome.

'My life is over,' I said.

Pia had frozen. 'What shall I do?'

'Come with me,' I said. 'I need you.'

Feeling like a prisoner walking towards his executioner, I made my way towards them. *Goodbye to the fundraiser, goodbye to my love life*, I thought.

'Jess, Pia, I'd like you to meet the Lewis family,' said Dad. 'This is Mrs Lewis and her children, Alisha and Jerome.'

Alisha muttered something and looked away.

Mrs Lewis put her hand out and shook mine and then Pia's hand. 'Pleased to meet you, girls.'

Jerome smiled at us. Up close, he was even more gorgeous, with deep brown eyes and astonishingly white teeth. 'Hey, Pia, Jess. Good to meet you and hey, no-one calls me Jerome. Please call me JJ.'

'Why JJ?' I asked.

'Jerome Junior,' he replied. 'JJ.'

'Alisha?' said Mrs Lewis, turning to her daughter.

'Later,' she said and flounced off towards the lift.

A look of irritation crossed Mrs Lewis's face. 'You'll

have to excuse Alisha. She, er . . .' She looked at Dad and shrugged her shoulders. 'Teenagers, huh?'

Dad gave me a pointed look. 'Indeed, you never know what they're going to do next.'

Oh God, he does know I was in the pool, I thought as I smiled back weakly.

Mrs Lewis sighed. 'Tell me about it.'

'You both go to school near here?' asked JJ.

Pia nodded. She'd done her frozen act and now seemed to have lost the power of speech. I wasn't sure what to do or say, either. Apologise about last night? Say I wouldn't do it again? But so far, no-one had said anything about it so I decided to stay schtum. *JJ must be so impressed by our brilliant conversation*, I thought.

'They both attend West Bailey High,' said Dad, who seemed amused by our silence. 'It's a good school only a bus ride away.'

'How about you?' I finally managed to blurt.

'We're home-schooled when we travel,' JJ replied, then flashed an award-winning smile. 'Which is why it's so nice to meet people like you.'

Pia let out a high-pitched nervous laugh.

'Ditto,' I said.

'Well, I hope we'll see some more of you around the place,' said Mrs Lewis. 'Lovely to meet you.'

'And you,' I said. It felt like meeting the Queen and I wondered if I ought to curtsey.

She smiled, then went off with JJ.

'She's nice,' said Pia. 'And so beautiful. She looks like Halle Berry. Did you see her skin? It's flawless.'

'Yeah,' I said. 'Shame her charm hasn't rubbed off on you know who.'

Dad indicated Reception. 'You may as well go through this way,' he said, 'seeing as you're here.'

I didn't need telling twice. Was I in the clear? No-one had said anything about the pool.

'And have a good time tonight, Jess,' he called after me. 'Don't be late back.'

I turned, stood to attention and saluted him. From the area where the residents' lifts were situated, I saw JJ watching and laughing. Behind him, Alisha was also watching, but the expression on her face was sulky.

'He loves me,' I said to Pia as we pressed the exit button to the staff area and went through.

'Yeah right,' said Pia. 'Dream on, girl. That boy oozed natural charm. I reckon he's like that with everyone. And, anyway, what about Tom?'

'Options, Pia,' I said. 'A girl has to have options and anyway, I can dream, can't I?'

An hour later, we were blow-dried, perfumed, made-up and dressed. Dad dropped in to see us before we went to catch the bus and he wasn't at all pleased to see me wearing make-up.

'You don't need it,' he said as he took in Pia's and my appearance. 'And you're both going to freeze in those outfits.'

Pia was wearing a wraparound green dress with a crocheted top that she had bought in the sale at TopShop during the holidays. She looked amazing. I'd tried on a million outfits and nothing looked right. My strapless flowery dress looked OK, but it was well into autumn now and I still looked like I was dressed for the summer. In the end, I settled for skinny black jeans and a red-and-black striped top that I'd had for ages. I really needed some new clothes. I'd been meaning to ask Dad all week, but it had never been the right time. I had to pick my moment.

'We're going to take jackets and scarves, Dad,' I said. 'We're not totally brain dead.'

Pia did a stupid face. ''Ot totally – ug still goh haf a bran.'

Dad sat on the end of my bed. He appeared distracted. 'No. Of course not. I . . . er . . . wanted to talk to you about something. Mrs Lewis asked to have a word with me before . . .'

My stomach sank. *Here it comes*, I thought. *What a waste of dressing-up time.*

'Before you say anything, I'm sorry and I won't do it again,' I said. 'I promise.'

Dad looked puzzled. 'Do what?'

Could it be that he doesn't *know about last night?* I wondered. 'I . . . Oh. Whatever it is I've done now.'

Dad laughed. Over his shoulder, Pia shrugged and made a face as if to say, I don't know what's going on either.

I decided to brave it out. 'Yes. That's my policy from now on, Dad. Apologise before I've done anything. Saves time and makes life a lot easier, don't you think?'

Dad chuckled then looked at me suspiciously. 'Maybe not such a bad philosophy but . . . you're not thinking of doing anything untoward, are you?'

'God no,' I said. I joined my hands in prayer and put on my best angelic look. 'Good as gold, that's me. Sister Mary Bernadetta Consuela Emmanuella bejesus begorah.' I broke into the nun's song from *The Sound of Music*. 'Climb every mountain . . .'

Dad regarded me for a few moments. 'You're a very strange girl, Jess Hall.'

I shut up.

'Anyway,' said Dad, 'before you go, I have a favour to ask of you.'

'Shoot,' I said.

'Mrs Lewis was pleased to have introduced you to Alisha and Jerome earlier on—'

'JJ, Dad,' I reminded him. 'Remember he said we were to call him JJ.'

'OK – then remember JJ said he and his sister were

home-schooled? Well, Mrs Lewis had a chat with me and said it concerns her that they're not getting to see the real London and asked if you might consider—'

'Showing JJ round? See, he *was* pleased to meet us, Pia. I told you!'

'No, not Jerome – I mean JJ – Alisha. Mrs Lewis is worried about having separated Alisha from her friends and wondered if you would show her a few places, maybe go shopping with her. Just be company for her.'

'Alisha? No way.' I pulled an 'I'm going to be sick' face.

Dad looked cross. 'Why? What's the problem? I'd have thought most girls your age would be delighted to have someone like her around.'

'Someone like her? A somebody, you mean?'

'Now come on, Jess. Where's that kind heart of yours? Yes, she's the daughter of a famous actor but she's also someone new to our city who probably needs a friend or two.'

'Let her go with them, then,' I said.

'Mrs Lewis mentioned a shopping expedition,' said Dad.

'I'll do it,' said Pia. 'Come on, Jess, it'll be fun.'

I shot her a filthy look then had an idea. Maybe this was my moment. 'Thing is, it would be awful, Dad. Can you imagine? They're loaded and I only have fifteen quid left in my savings account.'

'Ah, yes, about that. I was going to say. It's your birthday soon. How about I give you your present early? Rather than me pick something for you, I thought I'd give you cash so you could choose something yourself.'

Bribery! He had taken the bait. This was going *very* well. 'Maybe, but Dad, I don't think she likes me. You saw the way she flounced off before.' I wasn't about to fill him in on how rude she'd been to me nor where I'd bumped into her previously.

'It'd be a favour to me, Jess. I need to make a good impression. We all do. I'm sure you could take Pia along. I think Mrs Lewis wants Alisha to meet normal English teenagers.'

'Pia's not normal. She's mad. She was captured by aliens over the summer and they ate her brain.'

'It's true, Mr Hall, ergle burgle spoink,' said Pia, and she made herself go cross-eyed. 'It's very sad.'

Dad laughed and looked at me for my answer. I knew Pia wanted to go and she deserved a trip out to take her mind off the situation at home. Despite Mrs Carlsen's best efforts to find a new place for them to live, so far, she hadn't found anything suitable. I couldn't let her down.

'OK,' I said. 'We'll do it. It'll be difficult to pretend that we're normal, but we'll try.'

'And to make it up to you,' Dad continued, 'I was thinking that you could have a small birthday party here. Just a few of your girlfriends from school or the old neighbourhood. People you trust, of course, and who you can rely on to be discreet.'

It was getting better by the second. Already I was making a list. The kudos. A party at Number 1, Porchester Park. Strictly A-list. Everyone would want to be on it!

'Deal,' I said and put out my hand to high-five him. 'I will be the perfect tour guide.'

Pia gave me the thumbs up.

'What do you want to do on your birthday?' Pia asked as we took a last minute make-up check in the school cloakroom before going into the fundraiser.

'What do you think? The usual? Pizza. DVD, sleep-over?'

'Can you invite boys?'

'Doubt it. Dad said girls, didn't he?'

'Yes. Just . . . I wondered . . . with Henry living next door. He knows the rules at Porchester Park so would be cool, I'm sure.'

'And you love him even though you've only met him once.'

'I do. With a love that's true, which is why I need an opportunity to spend a bit more time with him. And Charlie will be there, won't he? Wouldn't he want a few boys for company?'

'Don't kid yourself, P. Charlie would love to be the only boy in a room full of girls. I'll ask Dad if we can have a few boys, though – Henry included – just for you. I can't stand in the way of true love, can I?'

On the way out of the cloakroom, we saw Tom and Josh coming along the corridor. Tom was looking gorgeous, dressed all in black. He looked right at me and smiled.

I checked over my shoulder to see if he was looking at someone else but no, the smile was directed at me. *Say something*, said a voice in my head.

'Mff,' came out of my mouth, as he approached.

'Hey. How's life in the fast lane, Hall?' he asked.

'Oh, same ol',' I said in my best casual voice. 'In fact, I was just chatting with Alisha and JJ Lewis before I came out.'

'JJ?' asked Josh.

'Jerome. His friends call him JJ,' I replied. 'They, er . . . want to hang out.'

'It's true,' said Pia. 'We're going shopping with them.'

'And will you be doing your zombie routine for them?' Tom asked as, on cue, Josh went into a zombie shuffle behind him. He bumped into Pia, who shoved him off in disgust.

'I only save that performance for special people,' I replied, and for a second, he looked right into my eyes and I felt a rush from my toes to the tip of my head.

He felt it too, I could tell, because his mouth curled into a half-smile. 'In that case, I'll consider myself honoured to have witnessed it,' he said as we got close to the assembly hall where the fundraiser was being held. 'God, I'm dreading this. Let's go in together, shall we?'

'OK, cool,' I said, and continued in a posh voice. 'One ought to have an escort when attending public events.'

'Or we could go in like the zombies in *Thriller*,' said Josh as he continued his zombie walk. *Some boys just don't know when to move on*, I thought, but Tom nodded and went into an excellent moonwalk à la Michael Jackson.

'Impressive,' I said, 'but you need to work on your facial expression. You look too normal.' I made my eyes cross and stuck out my tongue.

'Hmm. Sexy,' said Tom, and gave me a quizzical look.

Oops. Maybe some girls don't know when to move on, either, I thought as I immediately pulled my face straight. Sometimes I forget that boys like girls to be pretty and girlie.

Josh put his arm around Pia and squeezed her tight. 'And tonight's your lucky night, babe,' he said. '*You* can go in with moi!'

Pia shrugged him off. 'Dream on. I don't think my boyfriend would like it if he saw you trying to drape yourself around me.'

'What boyfriend?' asked Josh. 'I haven't seen you with anyone.'

'He lives at Number 1, Porchester Park,' said Pia. She looked at me to back her up.

'True,' I said. 'So back off or he might come after you.'

'Like I care,' said Josh, but he did let go of Pia.

As we went through the doors, on the other side of the room, Mrs Callahan, our headmistress, spotted us and began to make her way over.

'Ah, time to be bright and interesting and an example to the school,' said Tom. 'Here we go. Good job I do drama.'

'Er, yeah. Um, actually, before you go . . . I'm having a party in a couple of weeks time and we . . . we need a few spare boys. Strictly A-list, of course.'

'That would be me, then,' he said and he looked right into my eyes again, 'because there's someone there I'd like to get to know better.' My stomach did a double flip and as we walked across the hall, I could feel every girl in the room staring at us.

As I watched Tom go and chat to Mrs Callahan, I wondered if he had meant he'd like to get to know *me* better or one of the A-listers at Porchester Park. I so hoped that he'd meant me and wasn't using me to get in with the rich and famous.

The rest of the evening was a blur of chatting to

various parents and teachers, sipping lukewarm orange juice and handing around limp ham sandwiches. I didn't care. Every now and then Tom would glance over at me from across the room to check where I was and who I was talking to. Things were definitely looking up in the love department!

Later that night, I lay awake planning my birthday. Maybe eight people, maybe ten? Charlie, Henry, Tom . . . and I'd probably have to invite Josh, too. He told Pia that Tom had asked him for my phone number at the fundraiser. Huzzah. So. Pia, me, Flo and Meg would make up the girls. I knew I could count on them to be cool and I knew that Flo had a crush on Charlie so as well as being party hostess with the mostess, I'd also be matchmaker extraordinaire. Maybe the girls could stay over for my first Porchester Park sleepover. That would be cool. Maybe we'd have dancing. I would ask Charlie to put together a CD of romantic songs so we could all pair off.

I fell asleep with images of me and Tom in the courtyard, wrapped in each other's arms under the stars. He would look into my eyes, lean down towards me and his lips would . . .

Zzzz.

13

Living the Lux

'Where shall we take them?' I asked Pia as we stood at Reception the following Saturday morning, waiting for the Lewises to appear.

Pia shrugged. 'Westfield? TopShop? Everybody loves Topshop.'

I nodded. 'Or shall we stay local? Harrods. Harvey Nicks. Sloane Street? Flo suggested Notting Hill. She said there are some gorgeous vintage shops there.'

'Not sure. Alisha doesn't look like she'd be into vintage.'

'Will we take them on the tube?' asked Pia.

'God, I don't know. I bet Alisha's never been on a bus, never mind a tube. Dad didn't say how we get anywhere, just we've to take them around. Maybe I should run and ask him.'

Just then, Mrs Lewis and Alisha appeared from the lift and came over to us. I waved and Mrs Lewis gave us a bright smile, then went out to talk to a couple of middle-aged men who were hovering near a black Mercedes waiting out the front. Pia nudged me to look at the car while Alisha gave us the briefest of nods. I could see she was no happier with this arrangement than I was, but I smiled all the same. We didn't have to be besties. I was doing it purely like a Saturday job – like some girls wash their dad's cars, and others dig the garden, I act as a tour guide for my dad's posh residents. A girl's got to make a living and I was determined to do it well and to be friendly, a good example of a London teenager – besides, I liked Mrs Lewis. She had a nice open face and didn't seem snooty at all. Pia nudged me to look at Alisha's feet and I saw that as well as both wearing jeans, we were wearing the same coral-coloured Converse sneakers.

'Snap,' I said to Alisha.

'Meaning?' she asked.

I glanced down at our shoes. She looked horrified.

'We're wearing the same,' I explained.

'I can see that. But why snap?' she asked.

'It's a card game. Don't you have it in the States?' asked Pia. 'Each player has a pile of cards face down and you turn them over until you have a card that matches someone else's and then the first person to say "Snap" wins.'

'Whatever,' drawled Alisha, 'though we try to be individual where I come from.'

'Um . . . are we going in the limo, then?' I asked.

Alisha looked at me as if I was mad. 'How else?' She went out to the forecourt and got into the waiting car.

'Bus. Tube. Walk. Horse and cart,' Pia whispered to me.

'Whatever,' I mimed, and she giggled, followed Alisha and got into the car.

Didier winked. 'Your carriage, madam,' he said and held the car door open for me.

'Thank you, my man,' I said. I slid over to sit beside Pia. One of the men who had been chatting with Mrs Lewis got into the passenger seat. He was well-built with a closely shaved head and was dressed in smart casuals. I had seen him around a few times with the Lewis family and Charlie had told me that he was one of their minders. The other man got into the driver's seat. He was dressed in a suit, very Men in Black.

The back of the car could have comfortably seated six people and smelt of leather. I shot Pia a grin and settled back to enjoy the ride. The engine whispered into life and we moved off. *So far, so good. I could get used to this*, I thought, as I looked out. I just wished the people outside could see us living the lux, but the windows were tinted. We could see out but no-one could see in.

'Er, Pia and I weren't really sure where you'd like to go,' I said to Mrs Lewis. 'Dad said that we were to show you around a bit. Um. Pia and I like Westfield Mall and

TopShop and Selfridges has everything, but it depends on what you're looking for.'

'Mall?' said Mrs Lewis. 'TopShop? That's very sweet of you, Jess, but . . . no, not today. Too many people, you see, and . . .'

'We don't do anywhere with crowds,' drawled Alisha. 'We'd last five minutes and someone would be after us for a photo that they could sell to the papers.'

'Oh right, of course,' I said. 'I should have thought. Um. Harrods. No. Um. Probably too busy as well. Er . . . where would be best, then?' Inwardly, I cursed myself. I should have thought the trip through better. Of course they couldn't mingle like ordinary people. I should have asked Dad for ideas, but he'd been in such a hurry to get off to his office after breakfast, I hadn't had the chance.

'Don't worry, honey,' said Mrs Lewis. 'I have a few places in mind. They're expecting us and really, we just wanted your company. Alisha hasn't met many people of her own age here so far.'

I glanced at Alisha. She looked like she'd just sucked a lemon.

After about five minutes, the car stopped.

'What's up?' I asked Mrs Lewis. 'Did you forget something?'

Mrs Lewis shook her head. 'No. We're here.'

I glanced out. We were outside the shops at the

Knightsbridge end of Sloane Street. We could have walked the distance in almost the same time but after what Alisha just said about not being able to go out like ordinary people, I was beginning to get the picture.

In a flash, the minder was out. He checked the street, then opened the door for us.

'I'm Sergei,' he said. He sounded Russian. 'I'll be keeping an eye on you today. I von't ever be far avay but try not to vander off.'

'OK, Sergei,' I said. I liked the idea of having our own minder, very A-list. I couldn't wait to tell people at school. 'Though if anyone kidnapped me, I doubt they'd get much. In fact, my dad would probably pay them to keep me.'

Sergei chuckled. 'I'll keep zat in mind,' he said.

At the shop entrance, the beefy black doorman snapped to attention, whispered into his lapel radio mike and, seconds later, opened the tall bronze door to us with a smile. Pia and I trooped in with Mrs Lewis and Alisha, while Sergei followed discreetly behind.

As soon as we crossed the shop's threshold, a wave of slim, impeccably-dressed, young shop assistants surged towards us.

'Good morning, Mrs Lewis,' said a blonde one.

'Welcome. I'm Usha, head of personal shopping,' said a beautiful Indian girl. 'Do let us know if there's any way we can assist you and if you'd like to go to the private area.' She beckoned a girl with short dark hair forward. 'Anya will get you any refreshments you'd like.'

Anya stepped forward. 'Coffee?' she asked, in an accent I couldn't place. European. Not French. 'We presently have twelve blends,' she said, 'or would you prefer tea?' And she reeled off a list of teas and then soft drinks and water.

Mrs Lewis politely refused all offers and glanced at Alisha to see if she wanted anything. She shook her head. 'No. I'm ready to roll, Mom. Let's focus.'

Mrs Lewis turned back to the assistants. 'We'd like something for a special party,' she said 'But Pia, Jess, would you like something to drink?'

'Er . . .' I began. I'd have liked a Coke but I wasn't sure if that would be OK, seeing as Mrs Lewis and Alisha had declined.

Anya handed me a menu and smiled. 'Have a look and just let me know when you're ready.'

I nodded, took the menu, then Pia and I followed Mrs Lewis and Alisha, who were being ushered by Usha into a lift. *Usha the usher*, I thought and stifled a nervous giggle.

When we arrived at the personal shopper's suite on the second floor, Mrs Lewis settled herself on a grey velvet sofa and addressed the gathered assistants. I wasn't sure what to do with myself. I felt awkward and

I could see that Pia did too. I walked over to a display of shoes and studied them carefully so that I didn't look too stupid. Pia followed me and pinched my arm. In pinching language, I knew that meant, 'Argh, this is *so* uncomfortable.' I pinched her back to say that I agreed.

Behind me, I heard Mrs Lewis say, 'It's my daughter's birthday next month and she needs something really special.'

I turned to Alisha. 'Oh. Really? So you must be a Sagi.'

A flicker of interest registered on Alisha's face.

'Sagittarian,' Pia explained. 'Jess is too.'

Alisha raised an eyebrow, as if to say, so? She walked over to a rack of dresses and began flicking through them.

'When's your birthday, Jess?' asked Mrs Lewis.

'December third,' I replied. 'When's yours, Alisha?'

'November twenty-sixth,' she replied, without turning around. 'You're into astrology?'

'We like to read our horoscopes,' I replied, 'but I don't know much about it except that Sagittarians are supposed to be sporty and like travel.' I picked up a pair of high-heeled black sandals with a diamante strap. The price tag said £895. I put them down fast and picked up another pair. £1,450. 'Hmm, they'd be good for hiking.'

'We have our own astrologer back home, don't we, Mom?' drawled Alisha, as she flicked through another rail. 'Everyone in Hollywood consults him. He told me that no two Sagittarians are alike. It depends on your rising sign, your moon sign, where you were born, so . . .' she sighed heavily, 'though we might share the same birth sign, I doubt we have much else in common.'

'Except for your taste in shoes,' said Pia. She looked pointedly at our sneakers.

Alisha didn't reply and turned to inspect a handbag. I grinned at Pia and gave her a thumbs up. Not that I wanted to be like Alisha. I didn't like her attitude – like, we are so *not* alike, sister.

'What are you going to do for your birthday, Alisha?' I asked. I didn't suppose she knew many people in London yet so if she was nice to me, I thought that I might make an effort and invite her to my sleepover. I'd read somewhere that Sagittarians are meant to get on together and, given time, she might warm up.

'We're having a small party. About two hundred people, isn't that right, Mom? So my dress,' she took a long black evening dress that a smiling assistant handed her, 'has to be fabulous. I want it to be my Beyoncé moment. I want there to be smoke when I come out, like a diva. I want everyone at my party to want to be me.'

Pia and I glanced at each other. I knew what she was thinking.

'Two hundred! I wouldn't call that small,' she blurted.

Alisha shrugged and held a dress up against herself. 'Small by Hollywood standards.'

Mrs Lewis smiled at me. 'How are you going to celebrate yours?'

'Oh, nothing much. A few friends over. Sleepover maybe. No biggie,' I said. Alisha glanced over when I said the word sleepover. *Maybe I won't invite her after all,* I thought. *She'll think eight people is seriously small fry.*

'We'd love it if you and Pia were our guests,' said Mrs Lewis.

Behind her, I saw Alisha's expression harden. She dismissed the hovering assistant with a flick of her hand. 'We're done here,' she said.

'Um. I'll ask Dad,' I said. I didn't want to go to the party knowing that we weren't wanted, but Pia looked delighted by the invite.

'That'd be fabbie dabbie doobie,' she whispered.

The next few hours were a blur of shops with the same marble floor, the same lovely assistants, the same scented candles burning and the same way over the top price tags. Mrs Lewis, Pia and I watched Alisha try on a succession of wonderful dresses: silks, satins, voiles, lace. Prada, Dior, Chloe, Gianfranco Ferre, Dolce & Gabbana, Balmain – designers I'd heard of, some I hadn't, but none of the dresses were right for Alisha. I could see that clearly and, by the growing look of frustration on her face, so could she.

By the time we got to a small boutique just off Sloane Street, Pia and I were getting bored and I was feeling like a hanger-on. It certainly wasn't turning out to be as much fun as I'd imagined.

'How about *we* try some stuff on?' I suggested as Alisha took yet another stash of clothes into the changing area. 'Or else what are we going to tell Flo? You know how she loves clothes. She's so jealous we've been invited on this trip and if she finds out we didn't even try anything on, she'll be well disappointed.'

Pia nodded. 'Do you think we could?'

'Mrs Lewis, do you think we could try some clothes?' I asked.

'Sure you can, honey. Try what you like. In fact, I'm just going to go out for a short while, I saw some shoes earlier that are calling me back, so go right ahead. If you need anything, Sergei is over there.'

After she'd gone, we got straight on it.

'Let's pick one mad one,' I said. We picked five outfits each and were soon having a great time seeing how they looked. Pia looked divine in a long floaty Olsen twin number. I tried a Stella MCartney dress which, although lovely, made me look like a tall stick insect. Next, Pia slipped on a strange blue dress with a ruffled petticoat poking out underneath the hem. We couldn't stop laughing as she pranced around doing a mad ballet routine. I noticed Alisha watching us messing about, but when I glanced over at her, she quickly turned away. Sergei, on the other hand, appeared to be enjoying the show and cracked up. I chose a black leather warrior queen type dress and did some kung fu moves. Alisha rolled her eyes up to the ceiling. I didn't care. She took a red silk dress into the changing room and when she came out, she studied her reflection for a while.

'What do you think?' she finally asked.

It was all wrong for her. She looked like a kid in her mum's dress. I couldn't hold back any longer and pulled a face.

'Alisha, nothing you have tried on today has looked right,' I said.

'Oh, and you're some kind of expert, are you?' she said.

'Actually, she knows a lot about fashion,' Pia blurted out before I could defend myself. 'Her mum used to be a personal shopper, so she grew up learning the rules.'

'Which are?'

'Wear the dress, don't let the dress wear you,' I said, quoting one of Mum's favourites. 'You want people to notice you, not just what you have on. And, of course, money can't buy you style.'

Alisha looked at me as if I had sworn. 'Is that right?' she drawled.

Her attitude was beginning to annoy me. 'It's true. Um, like everyone knows that . . .' I searched my mind for something clever to say then remembered what Aunt Maddie had said over breakfast back at my gran's, 'that the West is, er . . . is steeped in materialism. Having it all doesn't make you happy. Some people have too much, in fact.' Even as it came out of my mouth, I knew I was voicing Aunt Maddie's ideas not my own. I would love to be stinking stonking rich, but I wanted to put Alisha in her place. I turned to Pia for agreement but from the look on her face, she clearly thought I'd gone too far.

Alisha laughed and flicked her hair. 'Some people have too much? It's true. And aren't I lucky that I'm one of them?'

'Er . . . not that I meant you, of course,' I stuttered. 'What I mean is . . . Oh, forget it. Listen. Do you know what kind of look you're going for?'

She shrugged a shoulder. 'I guess I'll know it when I see it. I always had personal stylists back home, but now . . .' Her voice trailed away.

'Why don't you let us help you? Pia and me are well into fashion. Like, do you want to look like a princess, a fairy, a rock chick? Do you like vintage, boho, indie, retro, goth? What's your style?'

Alisha shrugged the other shoulder. 'Not sure any more. I feel like I'm changing, you know . . .'

'Exactly,' I said. 'And that's great. You should never get stuck with one look that maybe worked once but not any more – plus our tastes change. So, OK. I'm going to be honest with you. That's a lovely dress. The kind of dress a top actress would wear to the Oscars. A *thirty*-year-old actress. You're going to be fifteen, right?'

Alisha nodded. 'Uh-huh.'

'Then I think you should go for something that suits your age. You've been trying all these faberoonie dresses but they're all way too old for you.'

'Excuse Jess,' said Pia. 'She sometimes speaks before she thinks. *Don't you*, Jess?'

'It's OK,' said Alisha. 'Actually, I like people to be honest.' She looked around at the assistants who were still hovering. 'I don't like people who suck up to me and I often feel that my mom's dressing me in the kind of clothes that she likes, so I can appreciate what you're saying. If my mom had her way, she'd have me looking like a Disney princess and that is, like, *so* last decade.'

'What would *you* like to wear?' asked Pia.

Alisha pulled a face and shrugged. 'I don't know any more. I feel like I'm . . . oh, never mind.' She suddenly clamped up as if she was annoyed with herself for having spoken to us at all.

I looked her up and down. 'You have great legs, Alisha. I think you should show them off. And I think . . . I think I saw a dress that would be perfect for you.'

I went back to the racks on the wall opposite, rummaged through and picked out a couple of dresses. I handed them to her.

'Try these. Short and sassy. They'd look fab. A pair of killer heels and you'll be the belle of the ball.'

She took the dresses and reappeared a couple of minutes later wearing a stunning, skin-tight black number with a glint of diamante in the fabric. Even she couldn't resist a smile when she saw her reflection.

'Wow!' Pia exclaimed. '*That's* more like it. Glam. Great cut. You look a million dollars.'

For the first time that day, Alisha smiled at us. 'Well played, peeps.'

'We'll get you some shoes,' I said. I was beginning to enjoy myself. 'When the going gets tough, the tough go shopping! Yay.'

Alisha high-fived me and we giggled like old mates. It seemed like the ice queen had finally melted and, for the next half-hour, Pia and I raced around picking out dresses and accessories for Alisha. We chose some stunning outfits for her and, for a short while, we got a glimpse of the girl behind the snootiness.

'We think we've found the perfect dress, Mrs Lewis,'

said Pia, when Alisha's mum reappeared just as Alisha was retrying the first dress.

'Alisha's putting it on now,' I said.

'Thank God,' she said, 'because my feet are killing me. Come on then, Alisha. Let me see.'

When Alisha stepped out of the changing room, Mrs Lewis's face dropped.

Alisha did a twirl. 'I just love this one, Mom. What do you think? Awesome, huh?'

Mrs Lewis shook her head. 'No. *No* way, Alisha. It's too short, too tight, too . . . *everything*.'

Alisha's mouth tightened.

'OK, let's not decide just now,' Mrs Lewis continued. 'Let's, er . . . I can have a few racks of dresses sent over and we'll decide later.'

'We'll come and help you choose if you like,' I offered.

Alisha ignored me and stomped back into the changing room. 'Now I have a headache, my stress levels have just rocketed. It's so unfair, Mom,' she called through the curtain. 'You never let me have what I want.'

When she reappeared, Mrs Lewis said that it was time we went home. As we were walking out, Pia spotted some tops at the front.

'Hey, there's that one we saw in Westfield,' she said. She went over and pulled out the silver top that we had seen weeks ago.

'Hey, yeah, that's the one,' I said. I held it up against myself. 'Nice, huh?'

'Are you going to buy it?' Alisha asked.

I shook my head. 'Duh. No way can I afford it.'

'Then I'll get it,' she said. 'OK, Mum?'

I couldn't believe it. My top. I glanced at the price tag. £500. It wasn't in the sale here. I was about to tell her she could get it cheaper at Westfield then I thought, *Why should I? She'll only think I'm a cheapskate*.

Mrs Lewis sighed. 'Sure, if you really like it, hon.'

Alisha looked over at the dress she had tried on. 'I'd rather have the dress.'

'No. It's too revealing,' said Mrs Lewis. 'But you can have the top if you really like it.'

Alisha stuck out her bottom lip and surveyed the room. 'This sucks,' she said, 'but if you're not going to let me have the dress that I want then I should have this as compensation.' She sounded so petulant. Suddenly she thrust the top back at her mother. 'Actually, forget it. I've changed my mind. I'm done here.' She glanced at me. 'I don't want a top that someone else has picked out.' She looked around. 'I don't think this party's going to happen.'

Pia and I glanced at one another. I couldn't help thinking what a spoilt brat Alisha was and how rude she was being to her mother. There were times I had been rude to my mum too. Times I'd flounced off like a princess and taken my moods out on her but I'd always been aware of how tight the dosh situation was and would never have thrown a strop like Alisha. As I watched Mrs Lewis hand the top back to the assistant, I felt a familiar lump come into my throat.

'I'd give anything to have even five minutes with my mum again,' I said.

'I know,' whispered Pia, and she linked her arm through mine.

There was an uncomfortable silence in the car going home until Alisha suddenly turned to us. 'I've been trying to think of a theme for my party and you've inspired one, Jess.'

'Cool,' I said. 'What's that?'

'Princesses and Paupers. What do you think, Mom? Some people could come in gorgeous dresses, others could come in rags. Wouldn't that be cool?' she said, then gave me a challenging look.

'Alisha, please!' Mrs Lewis snapped. 'Jess, Pia, I can only apologise.' She turned to her daughter. 'Young lady, you and me are going to discuss your attitude when we get back.'

Alisha looked unmoved. She sat there looking smug. What she had said had hurt – and she knew it. But I wasn't going to let her win.

'We could come as we are, then,' I said, and Pia burst out laughing.

'Yeah, we can do the pauper thing to a T,' she agreed.

'And anyway,' I added, as I remembered another of Aunt Maddie's favourite lines, 'everyone knows that money can't buy you happiness.'

Mrs Lewis nodded. 'Exactly,' she said and looked pointedly at Alisha.

'Pff,' snorted Alisha. 'Anyone who says that doesn't know where to shop.'

She was so brazen but actually, having seen the lovely clothes that I had today, part of me had to agree.

I looked at her hard. She looked back. It was like one of those stand-offs you see in cowboy movies. Eyeball to eyeball. Eventually she looked away. We weren't best buddies after the shopping session, we probably never would be, but I felt that she had gained some grudging respect for me. She had seen that Pia and I weren't losers who could be walked over, nor were we going to suck up to her.

When we got out of the car, Alisha stomped off towards the lift then suddenly turned and came back. 'Hey, you said that your mom used to work as a personal shopper, right?'

I nodded.

'Have her come and see us,' she said, then turned to her mother. 'That would be OK, wouldn't it?'

'No, actually it won't be—' I started.

'Oh, don't sweat it. She'll get well paid.'

'Money can't get you everything,' I said quietly as Pia instinctively moved closer to me as though to protect me.

Alisha flicked her hair back. 'I think you'll find that it can. Right, Mom?'

Pia linked my arm. 'Mrs Hall died nine months ago,' she said.

Mrs Lewis looked aghast. 'Oh Jess, honey. I am so sorry. I . . . we didn't know.'

Alisha's face went blank: it registered no emotion, not embarrassment, not regret. 'This is so messed up,' she said. She crossed Reception to the lift. The doors opened and she stepped in without waiting for her mother.

14
Unexpected Visitor

When I got home from the shopping trip I went straight into the kitchen to get a drink. I felt mad at Alisha for lording it over us, waving her status around. She was so stuck up, like she thought she was better than us. I hated her. And the way she had demanded that my mum should go and be her personal shopper! I wouldn't have let Mum go even if she *had* been alive. She'd have deserved better than being a servant for Princess Alisha. I felt tears threatening. *I am not going to let someone like her get to me*, I thought. *She's so not worth it. I don't even like her! She can take her swanky designer dresses and shove them up her bum, for all I care.*

I glanced out of the window and almost jumped out of my skin. A face was staring in at me. A very strange-looking face. Furry and flat, like someone had whacked it with a frying pan. It belonged to a white long-haired cat with enormous eyes. *Persian*, I thought. The cat tapped on the window with a paw and looked at me beseechingly. *Adorable.*

'Oh my God, you must be lost, baby,' I said, and I crossed the kitchen to open the window. In a flash, the cat was inside and leapt gracefully down onto the floor. It wound itself around my ankles, tail up in the air, and purred loudly. I picked it up and saw that there was a collar around its neck and a brass tag with a name engraved on it: Chu.

'Hello, Chu,' I said. 'I wonder if you're called that because you sneeze a lot. Ah chu!'

I heard someone come in the front door and Charlie appeared in the kitchen moments later.

He looked at the cat and then at me. 'Jess, are you *insane*? Where did you get that? Dad'll kill you!'

'The cat was at the window when I got home,' I said. 'He's not mine. He must have wandered in from somewhere. I think he's hungry.' I looked in the cupboards, found a sachet of Dave's cat food that had been left behind and put some in a bowl for Chu. He devoured it as if he'd never eaten before in his life, then looked at me expectantly.

'You can't keep him,' said Charlie.

I knelt on the floor and stroked Chu. 'I know that – I'm not stupid – but we can't leave him, either. It's freezing outside and it looks like it's going to rain. We'll tell Dad.'

Charlie went to the fridge, picked out a small bottle of berry smoothie and glugged it down. 'I'll go and find him,' he said, when he'd finished. 'You look after the cat.'

I took Chu over to the sofa in the sitting area, where he lay on his back and I tickled his tummy. 'Maybe fate sent you to me,' I said to him as he continued to purr loudly and nuzzle my hand. 'You're a nice boy, aren't you?'

Ten minutes later, Charlie arrived back with Dad, who looked harassed.

'I didn't steal him or anything,' I said. 'He must be lost. He just came here.'

Dad sighed heavily. 'Thank *God*. He belongs to the Mori family. Apparently he got out when there was a delivery.'

'The people who live upstairs?'

Dad nodded, while Charlie looked at me with sympathy.

'But I thought there was a no pet rule,' I said.

Dad looked embarrassed. 'For us, yes. Er . . . not for them. I . . . I'm sorry, Jess.'

I felt a ball of anger build inside me. 'That's so not fair,' I said as Chu hopped onto my knee, put his paws up on my chest and rubbed his nose against mine.

Dad nodded, looking around the room as if he wanted to escape.

'What about Mr Knight? He won't like it,' I said.

Dad sat on the sofa and stroked Chu. 'One set of rules for us, another for them. The residents can do what they like. The family have been frantic. They thought they'd lost him. We've had everybody out all afternoon looking for him. I was so worried that he might have strayed onto the road and been run over. Of course I'd have been held responsible.'

'Are you going to take him back?'

'I have to, Jess. I'll go and give Mr Mori a call now. He'll be very relieved. His daughter Sakura has been really upset.'

'Tell me about it,' I said.

Dad put his hand out and touched my arm. I flinched away. 'I know, Jess,' he said. 'It doesn't seem fair, does it?' He looked tired and, for a moment, I regretted having reacted the way I did. Dad sat back for a moment and laid his head against the top of the sofa. 'Before I go, how's your day been, Jess? How was your shopping trip?'

'Yeah,' said Charlie. 'Did you get me anything?'

'Nothing my pocket money would stretch to. Nothing under five hundred quid. Er . . . did anyone call when I was out?'

'Only someone for me,' said Charlie. I felt disappointed. I'd hoped that Tom might have phoned.

'Did it go OK?' Dad persisted.

'Do you want to know because you care about my

day, or because you want to check that I behaved well for your residents?'

As it came out of my mouth, I realised I was being just like Alisha. So much for not throwing a strop or being rude like her . . .

Then I thought, *But it's worse for me than it is for her. She's probably up there in her la-di-dah apartment right now having a bath in French perfume and drinking some posh juice freshly squeezed from fruits flown in from the other side of the planet, while here I am babysitting someone else's cat. It's not fair.*

'I want to know the answers to both my questions,' said Dad. 'I thought you'd enjoy hanging out with A-listers. Are you OK, Jess?'

I crossed my arms over my chest. 'Not really. It wasn't as much fun as I'd thought. Alisha acts like a spoilt princess.'

'You behaved though, didn't you?'

'*Me?* Hah. Yes, Dad. *We* behaved. Pia and I didn't let you down. Though you should ask Mrs Lewis how Alisha behaved.'

Dad looked at me, sighed again, then sat up and turned towards Charlie. 'How was *your* day?'

'Same ol',' he replied. 'Anyone want peanut butter on toast? I'm starving.' He went into the kitchen area. 'How about you, Dad? What's happening in La-di-dah Land?'

Dad rolled his eyes. 'Not so great. First that darn cat went missing and then there's a smell of fish coming from the hotel kitchen next door and it's permeating the lobby—'

'That's probably why Chu did a runner,' I interrupted. 'He smelt the fish.'

'Maybe, but it's not how we want a five star establishment to smell. All in all, it's not been a good day and on top of everything else, Poppy Harrington has quit. She's said she'll work to the end of the week and then that's it – but the book is full of appointments and there's no-one to organise the therapists.'

I felt so cross I didn't care. 'Maybe you should quit too. Then we could go and live somewhere else and have pets like normal people, and not have to live in a place with as many rules as a school or a prison.'

'Not an option, sweetheart,' said Dad. He got up wearily. 'I'd better go and let the family know about the cat and call the search off.'

When he'd gone, Charlie came back through. 'Take it easy on Dad,' he said.

'Why should I? He doesn't care about me,' I said. 'All he cares about is Number 1, Porchester Park.'

'You don't mean that.'

'Do.'

'Fine, act like a little kid, then.'

I stuck my tongue out at him. No-one understood. I hated my life. Chu came and nuzzled my hand again. It all felt so unfair. The richies could have pets but I couldn't and seeing Chu made me miss Dave more than ever.

When Dad reappeared, he was with a middle-aged, wiry Japanese man and a little girl of about nine who had her hair in two plaits. She was carrying a cat basket and looked as if she'd been crying. She put the basket down, ran over to me, picked up Chu and nuzzled into him and said something in Japanese. She looked up at me. 'Thank you much.'

'This is my daughter, Jess, and my son, Charlie. Charlie, this is Mr Mori and his daughter, Sakura,' said Dad.

Mr Mori nodded to me. 'Where did you find him?' he asked.

Although I was cross with Dad, I couldn't keep up the silent act with Sakura because she looked so distraught. 'He came to us. He was tapping at the window,' I said. 'I think he was hungry.'

'Mm. Sorry. No me speak good English. I try. Mm. Chu, he always hungry,' said Sakura, and her dad laughed. 'You like cat, Jess?'

I nodded and looked accusingly at Dad. 'I *love* them and you speak very good English, Sakura.'

Chu put out a paw and looked at me.

'You, he like,' said Sakura.

'I like him too.'

'Has girl sister. You like come meet one day?'

She looked at her dad and I looked at mine. Dad nodded, so I did too.

'I'd love to,' I said.

Later that night, as I snuggled under my duvet, I felt miserable. I hadn't even emailed Pia, Meg or Flo to tell them the latest. I didn't feel like talking to anyone. I felt angry with Alisha and Dad. I wanted Dave and Gran and things back to how they were. I had too many mixed-up feelings whirling around in my brain, I couldn't settle. *I don't like myself any more*, I thought. *I don't like what I'm feeling, like I've gone bad inside. I still worry about how I felt at Mum's funeral. It's like a black cloud that sits on my head, all the time. And now all this other stuff. I never used to feel like this. Jealous. Envious. Discontent. I never used to compare myself to other people, thinking they were better than me or had more than me or that I wanted what they had. Gran always says I should be grateful that I live in a country that has food and clothing. But I can't help it. I want nice things. I want world peace too. Of course I do, and for everyone to be happy, and I always get upset when I see the news and other people suffering . . . oh, I don't know. I am so*

CONFUSED. I never used to feel this way before. Should, shouldn't. Good, bad. Us, them. Upstairs, downstairs. Rich, poor. Me, her. I have to get out of here before I get totally bitter and twisted. I must. Before I go blooming mad.

15

Runaway

The invite to Alisha's party was delivered on Sunday morning, just as I was getting ready to go out to swimming practice. It came in a silver envelope lined with pink silk and was addressed to me and Charlie.

Carletta and Jefferson Lewis
are delighted to invite you
to their daughter Alisha's fifteenth birthday party.
On November 26th at 7.30pm.
Fifth floor, Number 1, Porchester Park.
Dress: Beauty and the Beast.
Carriages at midnight.
RSVP: 0207 776 5555

I read it slowly, taking in every word of the sweeping black script, then slipped the thick ivory card back into its envelope. No way was I going to go. Not after how Alisha had behaved on the shopping trip. *Girlfriend, you can take your posh invite and shove it where the sun doesn't shine*, I thought.

I went straight to Gran's after practice. When I'd packed my swimming stuff, I'd also put in my PJs and toothbrush so that I could stay the night. Hopefully Gran would drive me back to get the rest of my things later in the afternoon. Number 1, Porchester Park? I was outta there.

It was bliss to be back at the house, tea and Marmite toast in front of me, Dave curled up on my lap. I felt right again, like I was truly home.

'So, how's life back at the ranch?' asked Gran. 'What's the goss?'

I pulled a face. I didn't want to talk about it, or think about it, just yet. In fact, I wanted to put the place out of my mind forever.

'The lady who ran the spa escaped already,' I said.

Gran smiled. 'You talk about it as though it's a prison.'

I raised an eyebrow.

'You'll settle in,' said Gran. 'You just have to give it time.'

That's what everyone said when Mum died. Give it time. Time heals. All rubbish. I missed her as acutely now as I ever did. I tried to explain that to Gran.

'I know, love,' she said. 'Me too. So, what's your dad going to do?'

169

'About what?'

'The spa?'

'Oh, that. After he went into meltdown, he rang Pia's mum. She's over there now sorting out the rotas and booking therapists until he can find a replacement.'

'Of course,' said Gran. 'Wanda Carlsen's a force to be reckoned with, isn't she? If anyone can get that place organised, it's her.'

I nodded. I didn't really care. The whole place could go under and I'd be glad.

'Gran, can I stay over tonight?'

'Course you can, chicken. You'll have to sleep on the pull-out sofa, though, as I've put my studio back in order.'

'I . . . but . . .' I felt panic rising. 'I . . . er, that is, Gran . . .'

'Come on, spit it out.'

'I want to come back for good. Forever.'

Gran considered what I had said. 'But what about Charlie? And your dad? Your dad wants you with him.'

'He doesn't,' I blurted. 'He really doesn't. All he cares about is his job and what the smelly residents think of him. He has no time for me or Chaz.' I felt a pang of guilt when I remembered what Charlie had said about needing me to stay there with him. 'Charlie could come back too.'

'Is that what he wants?'

Reluctantly, I shook my head. I knew he liked having his own room. 'Not really, but it's different for him. He can shut things out better. He spends all his time with his music mates – apparently some new guy's joined the band who's really good, so he's got that to distract him.'

Gran came and sat on the end of the sofa and patted my leg. 'OK, tell me everything,' she said.

I started to fill her in on the last few weeks and when I got to the shopping trip with Alisha, and the episode with the cat, I felt a rush of anger. 'It's so not fair, Gran. I miss Dave. You know how much I love him, yet the residents can have exactly what they want and . . . well, it's not just that, although it is that, it's . . . oh . . . I don't know. I hate them but I'm beginning to hate myself more. I'm so mixed up. I don't know who I am any more. I don't like them but I feel jealous and angry and, oh . . . a whole load of other stuff I've never felt before. I don't like who I'm becoming. I'm thinking mean thoughts and feeling resentful all the time. I feel bad inside. Wanting what they have but not wanting it at the same time – like wanting to swim in their fabbie dabbie pool: it's ruined going to the public one for me, whereas before I never even thought about it. Now all I can see is how dowdy it is and how crowded and cold it is, but I have to go there to practise regularly as the school competition is next month. I can't swim in the spa – I'm not allowed.

Although I *have* been invited to Alisha's party, like rent-a-friend. So I'm allowed to be with them when it suits them. I just don't fit in there and yet everyone at school thinks everything's so fab and I'm so lucky and it's like I have to keep up this pretence that I'm living the dream. Like, yeah *right*. It's a total nightmare.' I burst into tears. 'I hate my life. I hate Dad. I hate living there. I want to come home and be with you and Dave.'

Gran moved down the sofa and took me in her arms and let me cry. She didn't say anything, just stroked my hair until the tears turned to sobs then finally subsided.

'And now I feel stupid. Blubbing like a big baby. I hate myself. I want to be normal again.'

'Hey. We all have times when we feel like a good cry,' said Gran. 'Does you good, I think. Gets it all out. I know it's been a hard time, a big readjustment, so of course you'll be feeling all sorts of new things. That's what life is like, Jess. New challenges. Nothing stays the same. Life moves on like a river, taking you with it, and sometimes it rushes by, and sometimes it flows sedately and gives you time to catch up – you just need time, Jess. You could never go bad inside, my love. It's not who you are and, trust me, I know.'

'So can I come back?' I whispered, through the sobs.

'Oh, Jess, I don't know—'

'Please. *Please*. You don't even have to let me have

your studio again. I'll sleep down here on the pull-out sofa. Please let me.'

Gran sighed and pulled me to her. 'If that's what you really *really* want, but we'll have to talk to your dad about it.'

Gran came back with me to the apartment block. She phoned ahead to tell Dad that she was coming and that I needed to talk to him. Charlie was out but Dad was waiting for us in the house, hovering nervously at the breakfast bar in the kitchen area. He looked worried.

'What's this all about?' he asked, when we came through the door. 'Has something happened? Are you all right, Jess?'

'She's fine, Michael,' said Gran. 'At least, not hurt but . . . Jess, do you want to tell him?'

'Tell me what? What's going on?' asked Dad.

I took my jacket off, but Gran kept her coat on.

'I'm going to leave you two alone,' she said. 'I'll pop out and pick up a few things for tea.'

She closed the door behind her and I turned to Dad. For a moment, I felt sorry for him. He looked so anxious.

'What's happened, Jess? Is it something at school? Are you being bullied?'

'No, nothing like that, Dad,' I said. 'Um, let's sit down.'

We went and sat on the sofa and Dad waited for me to speak.

My mind had gone blank. 'I . . . er . . . OK, I'm just going to come out with it. I . . . I want to go back and live with Gran.'

Dad's expression was one of relief. He breathed out heavily. 'Is that all?' He wiped his forehead with the back of his hand.

'I thought . . . I thought you'd be cross.'

'Cross? No. Not cross, Jess. Sad. But . . . I didn't know what to think when your gran called.'

'What *did* you think?'

Dad shrugged. 'Er . . .'

'Pregnant? On drugs?'

'Not exactly . . .'

'Dad! You *did*, didn't you? Actually I'm pregnant with twins – no, triplets! Impregnated by an alien, so they'll be extraterrestrials.'

Dad smiled wistfully. 'Honestly, I didn't know what to think. Your gran sounded so serious. I knew something was up. I . . . I was worried. So, you want to leave?'

I nodded. 'Can I?'

He didn't say anything for a while. 'Why do you want to go?'

I didn't feel that I could talk to him the way I had to Gran. 'All sorts of reasons. I feel at home with her.'

Wrong thing to say. Dad looked so hurt and then sad again. God, life was difficult sometimes.

'Jess, if you're unhappy here then of course I won't stop you. All I care about is your happiness.' He sighed. 'I've let you down, haven't I?' He looked around. 'You don't feel at home here?'

I shook my head. 'It's all so new.'

Dad nodded. 'For me, too. Every aspect of it. I don't think I got how twenty-four/seven this was going to be and . . . well, I'm sorry if I've neglected you. It won't always be like this. Things will settle as the staff find their way. It's like a new term at school. Remember how you hated it when you started secondary school?'

'God, yes. It felt so enormous after junior school and I kept getting lost and couldn't find which class I was supposed to be in.'

'Exactly, I remember your mum telling me how you pretended to be sick for weeks . . .'

'I even painted my face green one day, but of course Mum just cracked up instead of being sympathetic.'

'You could never fool her. But you know the place like the back of your hand now, don't you?'

'I guess.'

'It could be the same here if you gave it time. Jess, we're family. We should be together.'

'Gran's family too. Her house is the family house. It's . . . it's like a link to Mum.'

Dad breathed out heavily again. He looked so tired. 'You must miss her a lot.'

I nodded. 'I do,' I whispered. I wondered how it had been for him. We had never spoken about it, but they had been married for sixteen years and had stayed in touch so they must have loved each other once. 'Why did you and Mum really split up, Dad?' I asked. I remembered them sitting down with Charlie and me and giving us some story about how they loved us but couldn't live with each other any more. Same ol' schpiel all my mates whose parents had split up got. 'Was there someone else?'

Dad hung his head. 'Not someone else.' He gestured outside to the towering apartment block behind us. '*Something* else. My job. The strange hours of working in a hotel. Working for the kind of people who want you on call. Your mum was right. I wasn't there and she'd had enough of having an absent husband. And now it seems I'm doing it again, being an absent father.'

'No. Not really. It's OK.' I hated seeing him like this – and him not being around wasn't the only issue. 'Mum always said that being ill made her realise what was important in life.'

'Which is what?'

'Friends. Family.'

'Of course,' said Dad. 'Family. She always put you two first.'

'She also said that she felt that life had dealt her a double-sided card. On the one side, she had her family and a great life and on the other, every time she went to the hospital there was a reminder that she was just passing through this world. That we all are. Nothing is forever.'

'That's very deep for a fourteen, soon to be fifteen-year-old girl.'

'That's me. Deep,' I said. I grinned at him. 'Mum said I was deep too. She always spoke very openly to me about what was going on and what she was thinking.'

'What else did she say?'

'That in one way she was grateful that she had time to say goodbye and to put everything in order. Some people just die. *Poof* – they're gone. I don't know which I think is best. Like, when Charlie and I were kids, we used to ask each other: Would you rather be burnt to death or drown?'

Dad rolled his eyes. 'What a question! What a morbid pair of kids you are.'

'Not really,' I said. 'Everyone used to ask each other stuff like that. Like, would you rather be blind or deaf? Stuff like that.'

Dad didn't seem to be listening any more. 'She was very brave,' he said, finally.

'She was,' I replied. 'Where do you think she's gone? I don't understand how someone can be here one day, then gone the next, never to return. Where do they go?'

'I wish I knew,' said Dad. He reached over and put his hand over mine. I turned mine over and held his hand properly and we stayed like that for a short while.

'I . . . I always wondered, Dad . . . on the day of the funeral . . . why did you leave so soon after?'

Dad sighed. 'I couldn't handle it. I could see you and Charlie were OK with your gran and Aunt Maddie and I just needed some time out, on my own, you know? I had so many mixed-up feelings.'

I nodded. I knew all about mixed-up feelings.

'I'm afraid I went home, drank far too much and bawled my eyes out as I remembered the better times. I did love your mother, you know. It felt so unfair what happened to her and, well, there was so much left unsaid between us.'

'I hated that day,' I said. 'I wish I could have cried but I couldn't – that is, not on the day.' I wondered whether to tell Dad my secret. Would he understand? 'I . . . I got all confused – like, remember those neighbours of ours: the Petersons?'

Dad nodded. 'Oh God, that pushy couple! Yes, your mother disliked them, they were always showing off about everything.'

I took a deep breath and suddenly it felt like I *had* to tell him. To tell *someone* at last. It was like a huge wave bursting through a wall and there was no holding it back. 'Well, they were there at the funeral and they bagged a place on the third row. The *third* row. I was so mad with them because there were loads of people at the back that Mum had loved who had to stand and there were the Petersons sitting proud as punch in prime seats, like old ladies at a hanging, taking it all in. All the tributes and the hymns. Even one of Mum's cousins, Heather, had to stand at the back and she and Mum were really close. I felt so *angry* and all I could think about was how mad I was and how Mum never liked them anyway and then I thought I was the worst person in the world for thinking such bad thoughts in a church. Mum wouldn't have liked that and they probably didn't mean any harm and then I didn't know *what* I was feeling, I only knew that I couldn't cry. Not then. I've felt *terrible* about it ever since, like I didn't even cry at my mum's funeral because I was so busy being cross and judging people. Charlie cried. Aunt Maddie cried. Gran did. I didn't. How bad is that? It eats away at me. Instead of grieving for Mum, I was thinking hateful thoughts about people who probably meant well. I am the meanest, worst person in the world.'

'Oh no, Jess. Not at all!'

I felt like I was going to cry again. 'I *am*. I'm a horrible person. I hate myself . . .' I couldn't say any more. I felt a wave of emotion rising up from the pit of my stomach and tears spilt down my cheeks. My head ached and my chest hurt. The tears seemed to be coming from a bottomless pit inside of me and I had to take great gulps of air in order to be able to breathe.

Dad put his arm around me, cuddled me to him and let me cry into his chest. 'And you've been carrying this around all this time?' he asked, when finally the flood had subsided.

I nodded. 'And now I don't seem to be able to *stop* crying!' *What is the matter with me?* I thought. 'Am . . . *am I* the worst person in the world?'

'Not at all. Not at all,' he said and he held me close. It was a long time since Dad had cuddled me and I felt like a little girl again, safe in his arms, breathing in his familiar Dad smell.

'Grief is a curious thing,' he said, after a few minutes. 'Sometimes when you can't handle what you're feeling, your psyche throws up an emotion that you *can* handle instead. I think the pain of losing your mother was too much for you – no girl your age should have to bury their mum – and what happened was that part of you threw up a feeling that you *could* handle: anger, and you went with that. Quite understandable. In a way, your anger was protecting you from the deeper feelings that were too much that day.'

It kind of made sense. 'So I'm not a bad person, then?'

'Not at all. Not one bit. And the Petersons should

have had more respect, more sensitivity. They should have stood at the back and let your mother's close relatives take the seats.' Dad suddenly grinned mischievously. 'Hey – you know what you were saying about friends and family being important?'

'I know and I am sorry I don't want to stay here. I . . . I know you want me to but—'

'I do want you here, of course I do, you're my daughter and I love you but, as I said, your happiness comes first . . . But I may just have something that might tempt you to stay . . .' He had a mysterious twinkle in his eye.

No way, I thought, as I sat up and wiped my eyes. *Nothing on earth will tempt me to stay, not even having cosy chats like this with you.* Although I couldn't deny that it had been nice and I did feel closer to him than I had in ages.

'OK, shoot,' I ventured.

'It has to be a secret. Not a word to anyone.'

I made the zipping my lips gesture with my index finger and thumb. 'I told you mine, so you tell me yours.'

'You know how Pia's mum has been round sorting out the mess in the spa?'

I nodded.

'Well, we got chatting before you came back. She's done a first class job—'

'Mum always rated her.'

'Well, she was telling me about her work situation and how things have been tough for her of late, so . . . I've decided to offer her the job.'

'You mean running the spa?'

'I do. As you know, it comes with a house, so with her current difficulties I can't see how she can refuse so, if she accepts the job, she'll be—'

'Oh my God! Living here!' I felt a rush of hope. 'And so would Pia.'

Dad nodded.

'Oh my God,' I repeated. Visions of Pia living next door to me flooded into my brain. Going to school together. Getting the bus back.

Having her at Porchester Park would change everything. It wouldn't be me against the world. It would be *us*. Mates together. I could survive anything if only I had her close by to talk to and share everything with.

'Might that change your mind?'

'That would be totally *totally* fantastic.'

'Not a word to anyone, just in case Mrs Carlsen doesn't accept.'

'Not a word,' I said.

As soon as Dad had gone back to work, I got out my phone and dialled Pia.

'Hey, Jess—' she started.

'You will never *believe* what I am going to tell you.'

16
Party Time

As soon as Pia opened the front door, I could smell the lovely familiar scent of her mum's herbal potions.

'You've done a great job settling in,' I said, as I looked around the new house. It had only been a few days since they'd moved in, but Mrs Carlsen had already done her Queen of Organisation act and got the place spick and span.

It had been perfect timing all round. I knew that Pia had been worried about where she and her mum were going to live when their lease expired, and I had been worried too, in case they moved further away – so it felt like a fairy godmother had waved a magic wand for all of us, getting Mrs Carlsen the spa job. Having Pia as my neighbour had totally changed how I felt about being at Porchester Park, and I had told Dad that I would stay. I also felt like a huge weight had lifted since sharing my secret about the funeral with him. Maybe one day I'll tell Pia about it too, though not yet. What I'd told Dad was just between him and me and I knew that he understood completely.

'So, what do you think about going to this party?' asked Pia, eyeing a familiar silver envelope on the desk in her bedroom. 'I've been invited now, and so has Henry, and with you and Charlie as well, there'll be four of us against them.'

I picked up the invite and turned it over in my hand. It was Pia's first week at Porchester Park – how could I say no to her after all that she'd been through recently? Plus, if she was going, it might actually be fun. 'I suppose it *would* be a shame to miss a party like that.'

'Yeah – and you know how I love a chance to dress up,' she said.

I grinned. 'Shame Alisha didn't go for the pauper theme, though. We could have Versaced up a black bin liner with some safety pins.'

'That's my girl,' said Pia. 'So. What *are* we going to wear?'

Over the next week, we spent hours trying to find the perfect outfit. We went over to Gran's and rummaged through her old dresses, hoping for something vintage and original. Nothing looked right. Then we went through Pia's mum's evening clothes. A posh trouser suit and a black velvet dress. Not right for a teenager. We went to Flo's, but all her clothes were floaty and girlie, not mine or Pia's style at all. We didn't bother going to Meg's, as we knew her wardrobe would be full of jeans, T-shirts and sneakers, not posh party wear. By the end of the week, we'd tried on every stitch of clothing we had between us but there was still nothing suitable. There were going to be so many amazing outfits at the party – how could we even hope to compete?

'We're going to stand out as a real couple of losers,' I said gloomily, as I looked at myself in a pair of old black trousers and a red tunic top. The outfit looked so shabby in comparison to the dresses we'd seen Alisha trying on in Sloane Street. 'I saw a van arriving last night and rails of clothes being wheeled through the lobby to the lift. Going up to Alisha's, I bet,' I sighed.

Pia did the L for loser sign on her forehead. '*You* can be a loser but I re*fuse* to talk that language. Loser is a state of mind. Maybe Flo could make us something. She did some great stuff for the school fashion show last Christmas.'

'Maybe,' I said. I couldn't raise any enthusiasm. I had been one of Flo's models at that show and everything had looked wrong on me. Her clothes were OK – romantic, like her – but they were for waifs with no boobs or hips, and I had both.

'Maybe Alisha will go as a beast,' said Pia. 'Sexy beast, type of thing.'

'She's certainly beastly enough,' I replied.

'Arf, arf,' said Pia. 'Tu es très amusant ce matin.'

The following morning, Dad had to pick up something for a resident from somewhere near our school, so he offered to give me a lift. On the way there, I told him of my dilemma, in the hope that he'd write a big cheque so that I could go and buy a Dior original. Fat chance, I knew, but a girl can dream.

'I was talking to Mrs Lewis yesterday about the arrangements for the party,' he said, as we wound our way through the traffic. 'She says that some people are really going to town on the theme and taking it very literally – so it's not just a chance to wear a posh frock but to do something really creative. There's your opportunity to think outside the box, Jess. Be original, individual. Have some fun with it! You don't want to go looking like everyone else. You've worn some amazing fancy dress in your time. Remember when you went to Pia's party dressed as one of the Daleks from *Doctor Who*? Why not go down to a fancy dress hire shop? I reckon I could stump up for a costume of sorts for you and Charlie.'

'I was ten, then,' I replied. 'So I don't think so.'

As we continued on our way, I searched my mind for a unique idea. Something so brilliantly eye-catching that JJ couldn't fail to notice me in it. Nothing had happened with Tom after the fundraiser apart from the occasional glance when we passed in the school corridor, so I had decided to turn my attentions to JJ. If I got off with him, that would show Tom! But what should I go as to impress JJ? Beauty or the beast? Dad had got me thinking.

Then it hit me. *We're going to do this party in style*, I thought, as Dad dropped me off at school. I couldn't wait to tell Pia my idea.

On the night of the party, Charlie, Henry, Pia and me made our way through Reception to the desk and across to the lift where a couple of ushers dressed in black and white greeted us. Dad had advised us to wait until everyone else had arrived and to go up when the party was already buzzing, rather than being the first people there and standing around like limp lettuces.

'Time to be fashionably late,' I said, as I checked my watch.

One of the ushers bowed and pressed the button for the lift. He didn't bat an eyelid at our costumes.

'Probably seen people dressed as all sorts of beasts and ghouls going up,' Pia said.

'Mff,' I mumbled from under my snorkel. We caught sight of ourselves in the mirrored walls of the lift and burst out laughing. Charlie and Henry looked hysterical. Both had dressed up as beauties and were kitted out in full drag. Charlie was a Scottish lady in a kilt, his orange curly wig topped with a tam o'shanter – a red tartan beret – which he'd paired with red tights, yellow wellies and a ton of make-up. Henry had gone for a more traditional beauty and had blinged up in a full footballer's wife outfit – long blonde wig, white dress and a pair of size ten white high heels he'd got from somewhere. He was clearly having difficulty standing in them, because he flopped his feet over to rest on the outer sides. He tossed his golden tresses to show off chandelier-sized diamante earrings. 'Subtle, don't you think?'

'Very,' I replied. 'And your dress. It's so—'

'Revealing? Oh hell,' he said, adjusting his bra, which he'd stuffed with a pair of football socks. One 'boob' had slipped, so the other looked twice the size. 'How do you manage these things?'

'You could have shaved your legs,' said Pia, when she glanced down at his hairy calves.

'Dahling,' he said in a high voice, 'I prefer the natural look.'

'And that's why you've applied your make-up with a trowel and have a ton of red lipstick on your lips and cheeks?' said Pia. 'Very natural. Not.'

'Balance, dahling, balance,' he said, then dropped his voice down to a more normal pitch. 'But honestly, I don't know how you girls walk in these shoes.'

Pia and me had gone for the beast look. I was the Loch Ness monster. I was wearing a pale grey wetsuit, black flippers and a pair of goggles over a fish facemask. I looked truly beastly. Pia had gone for the ghoul look and was wearing a Victorian nightdress which she now buttoned over her head so that it looked like she was headless. Under her arm, she was carrying a false head that dripped fake blood. The only way she could see was by peeping through the buttons in the nightdress and groping with her hands. I thought we looked terrific. It was going to be a great laugh seeing what other beasts were there and loads more fun than trying to be a beauty on a budget.

The lift reached the lobby of the party room floor and, as the doors opened, we minced, tottered and flopped past a trio of ushers in the same black-and-white uniforms as the ones downstairs. One took our party invite and checked our names against a long list. Another bowed and offered us a drink off a silver tray. Henry took one of the champagne flutes and held it by its twisted silver stem next to Pia's false head – even the waiter had to laugh. I took a sip of my pink drink. It tasted divine: passionfruit and mango. Lovely.

Henry asked for a straw so that Pia could drink through the gap in her nightie. She took a slurp as an usher opened the double doors to the main room and the party.

'Miss Jess Hall, Miss Pia Carlsen, Mr Charles Hall and Mr Henry Wade,' he announced in a loud, posh voice.

We stepped into a glittering room already crowded with guests mingling and chatting. The room had been transformed into a white and silver grotto. I felt like I'd walked onto a movie set. A few people turned to see who had just come in. They froze, eyes wide, jaws dropping. I heard laughter to our left. And then silence as the rest of the guests turned and stared.

I spat out my snorkel. 'Oh. My. God,' I said, as I peered through my goggles, which were beginning to steam up from my breath. I could see that we'd got it thoroughly, disgustingly, mega wrong. Everyone else looked glamorous with a capital G – the room was a sea of diamonds and designer dresses. Dad had got it totally wrong when he had said that people were going to be creative. There wasn't a wacky fancy dress outfit in sight, whereas we looked like we'd just escaped from a cheap joke shop.

Pia was clearly having difficulty seeing at all and walked into a wall. 'Er . . . Oops,' she said, as Henry steered her back towards the party.

'Don't let her wander off,' he said. 'She might walk into a table full of food.'

'Look at the guests,' I whispered. Pia peered out from a space between nightdress buttons. Most of the girls had come as beauties, with fabulous frocks, glittering jewels and killer heels. The boys were dressed in suits mainly, although a good number of them had gold or silver Venetian carnival masks on and a few had red horns on their heads. All very elegant and tasteful.

It was so different to the last time I had been up in this room to meet the staff – they'd been dressed in ordinary clothes, the refreshments had been few and far-between and the decorations non-existent. This time, everyone exuded glamour, the room had been transformed into winter wonderland – like a Snow Queen's palace – and everywhere you looked there were huge vases filled with hundreds of white-stemmed roses. The lighting was soft and an army of waiters and waitresses were taking around drinks and silver trays full of enticing-looking canapés.

'Wall-to-wall beauties,' giggled Pia, as she peeped out at the guests. 'Oops.'

Mrs Lewis came forward with a smile plastered onto her face and peered at my mask and goggles. 'And who do we have under here?'

'Jess, Mrs Lewis – Jess Hall,' I said, as I tried to raise my mask a little but only succeeded in ramming my snorkel up my nose.

'Ah.' She looked at the headless nightshirt. 'And?'

'Pia,' said a shaky voice from under the blood-spattered white fabric. I could tell she was having a hard time not cracking up laughing.

'Hello, Mrs Lewis,' said Charlie.

Mrs Lewis looked across at the boys. She struggled to turn shock into a polite expression.

'Ah, Charlie and . . .?'

'Henry,' he said, in a girlie voice with a flick of his hair.

Mrs Lewis kept her smile fixed on her face. 'Well, what . . . what *novel* costumes. Er . . . have you got a drink? Do come and meet everyone.'

She beckoned us towards the other guests, most of whom were still gaping at us open-mouthed.

'Ohmigod. There's Kitty Bonard,' said Pia through her peephole. 'How does Alisha know *her*?'

I glanced over to see a stunning girl with long red hair in a scarlet dress. 'Who's she?'

'*Kitty*, you *know*. She does a piece in *Girl in the City* magazine. She does a brill blog on teen fashion.'

'She can say that wetsuits are in, then,' I said.

'And look! There's Marcus Flynn from last year's *Big Brother*. Wow. And – ohmigod, I am going to *die* – there, standing by the bar, that's Adrian Bailey.'

I looked over to see that not just Adrian but all his band mates from Cursed were watching us and laughing their heads off. They were the hottest boy band in the universe. I so wished I hadn't dressed like a prize idiot. I adjusted my goggles, thankful that at least no-one could see my face.

'How come Alisha knows them?' I asked.

'They're on a list,' said Henry. 'My dad told me. PR companies have lists of people who are in at the moment. They want to be seen and people pay to be seen with them. What do you think all those paparazzi were doing outside? It's PR heaven.'

Pia scoffed. 'Two hundred of your closest friends, none of whom you have actually met before.'

'Who cares?' I said. 'Two hundred people I'd really like to meet! I wonder if Cursed are going to play. That'd be awesome. Do you think we could slip away and change?'

'No way,' said Pia. 'We stand out in the crowd.' She undid her buttons and popped her real head out and tossed the false one onto a chair. She still stood out as she had plastered her skin with white make-up and used green lipstick. She'd also brought some plastic fake eyes which were bulbous with red veins and no eyelids. She put them in and looked hideous but it made me laugh so much that I had to pull my mask away from my face so that I could breathe.

'Want to put some eyes in? I brought a pair for you,' she asked as a male guest went past. 'Would you like some? I've only got eyes for yoo-ou.'

'I don't think so,' he replied snootily and hurried back to join his friends who were looking at us as if we were mad.

'Eyes, Jess,' Pia repeated.

I shook my head and fixed my mask back on properly. 'At least no-one knows it's me under here. We stand out for all the wrong reasons. I so wish I'd worn something pretty.'

'You could have worn Sakura's cat on your head,' said Pia. 'He's pretty.'

'Dad told me that Cursed *will* be playing,' said Henry, coming to join us again with more drinks. 'Cost a hundred grand to get them. Whole party cost over four hundred thousand.'

'Wow,' I said. Dad told me the budget on my party would be eighty quid. Pizzas, then ice cream for everyone, and I'd thought that was generous.

All around us, people were still staring.

'You going to take off your fish mask and snorkel and eat something?' asked Pia as a waiter passed by with a tray of bite-sized silver-and-white cupcakes.

'No way,' I said. 'I'm going to maintain my air of mystery.'

Pia laughed and took one of the dinky cakes. 'Er . . . the fact that we were announced might have been a slight giveaway,' she said, then popped the cake into her mouth. 'But I don't know what you're worried about. Who cares what this snobby stiff lot think? At least our outfits show that we have a sense of humour and are up for a bit of fun.'

Charlie and Henry didn't seem fazed by the reaction to their outfits and even seemed chuffed when one of the boys from Cursed wolf-whistled at them, plus they appeared to be attracting attention from a couple of leggy blondes who had sidled up to them. Not surprising really, because, even in drag, anyone could see that they were a couple of very good-looking boys and, strangely, they both looked pretty good in make-up.

I knew Pia was right about not worrying and I told myself to loosen up and get into the party mood. I tried to adopt a cool posture but it wasn't easy dressed in a wetsuit, flippers and goggles. I was boiling. All around me were people who had just stepped from the pages of a gossip magazine. A couple of teenage celebs walked past and tried not to laugh as Pia and I stood in the corner and took it all in. Curiously, no-one came over to chat to us.

'Where's Alisha?' I heard Charlie ask one of the blondes he was chatting to.

'Arriving any minute now,' she said. She indicated a wide screen above the bar area where there was live footage of the courtyard at the front of the apartment block. A couple of late arrivals were getting out of a limo and were being ushered through.

'Here she is,' someone called from the back and I looked up at the screen to see a white limo arriving at the front. Didier leapt to open the door and Alisha stepped out looking every bit the A-lister she was. She was wearing a stunning silver-and-white strapless evening dress and had a sparkling diamond tiara on her head. She looked beautiful – the belle of the ball – though I suspected that the dress, with its long, full skirt, was her mother's choice, not Alisha's. I wondered what was going through her head and if she'd given in happily in the end. Behind us came a sigh of admiration from the crowd. Next to me, Pia had slid down the wall laughing.

'Ohmigod,' she said. 'Now we're going to look more out of place than ever. Or should that be ohmicod, we're going to look out of plaice . . . Get it? Plaice, the fish.'

'I get it, Pia,' I replied. Somehow, I didn't find it as funny as she did.

Alisha looked up into the camera and waved. The guests waved back.

At the lift there was a sudden commotion and the tall door to the lobby closed.

'What's happening?' I asked.

'Grand entrance methinks,' Pia replied and, indeed, about five minutes later, a song with the words 'isn't she lovely' began to play.

'Stevie Wonder,' said Charlie.

'What? Is he here?' I asked.

'No, the song is by him, dingbat brain,' said Charlie.

'Though it's not an impossibility, as I heard that he's an old friend of Jefferson Lewis's.'

The lights went down and, from the back of the room, silver spotlights began to swirl around the room then fixed on the doors. The lights went up, the doors opened and we saw that two lines of boys dressed in gold and wearing lions' head were waiting by the lift. *Slightly more elegant beasts than my interpretation*, I thought as the boys rolled out a red carpet then began to dance to the music.

The lift door opened. Alisha stepped out and the dancers stood opposite each other, raised their arms and made an arch for her to walk through. They showered her with butterfly-shaped confetti, then separated out and escorted her into the party, dancing by her side. Beauty and the beasts. Perfect. Alisha looked radiant as she surveyed the crowd to see who was there. She beamed at the boys from Cursed, waved at Marcus Flynn who winked back, smiled at Adrian Bailey . . . and then she turned and saw Pia, Charlie, Henry and me. Her face fell. She looked questioningly at her mother, who just shrugged. Alisha turned to look at us again. Charlie and Henry still didn't appear bothered. In fact, they were both grinning at her like idiots.

'Happy Birthday,' said Charlie.

'You look like a Disney princess,' Henry gushed. A flash of annoyance crossed Alisha's face.

'Oscar de la Renta,' she said, while beside me, Pia did a barfing sound which Alisha didn't miss. She came towards us and pointed at me.

'Who's in there?' she asked.

'Jess,' said Henry. 'Her and Pia have come as beasts. We're the beauties.' He did a twirl and wiggled his hips and one of his football socks fell out of his bra.

'You don't say,' said Alisha. She paused a moment, looked Pia up and down, then finally looked at me. '*How* embarrassing,' she said and, with a flick of her hair, she turned and walked off towards the bar.

17

Cats

After half an hour of standing around at the party like an idiot, with no-one coming to talk to me, and Pia having a great old time chatting away with Henry, I noticed JJ dancing with a stunning leggy brunette in a red shimmery short dress. *That's it*, I thought. *Everyone's having a fab time apart from me. What was I thinking of, coming here dressed like a deranged idiot? Everyone must think our fancy dress idea is so juvenile and they're right. No wonder no-one's been over to chat to me, like, who'd want to talk to a monster fish? Not exactly every boy's fantasy! And if JJ does ever notice me, he'll put me on his list of people to avoid forever. I'd better get out of here quick before he realises it's me under here.*

I crept downstairs to change. Pia refused to give in and come with me so I left her with the boys. It was all right for her. She didn't look too bad with her white make-up and Victorian nightdress – at least she looked more like a naughty cherub than a monster. If I'd taken off my snorkel and fish mask, I'd have looked like some mad person in a wetsuit who'd wandered in from snorkelling school by mistake.

I put on my black trousers and red-and-black striped top, then made my way back over to the lift in the Reception area. I saw Sakura waiting with a Japanese lady. She introduced me to her mum, who didn't speak very good English but smiled at me and nodded.

'You going Lewis party?' asked Sakura.

'I am.'

'Lucky you,' said Sakura.

The lift arrived and we stepped in.

'Hey,' said Sakura. She pointed upwards. 'We up above party floor. You want come meet cat sister?'

'I can't think of anything I'd rather do than meet cat sister,' I replied. It was infinitely preferable to going back to the party, where I'd probably just be standing on my own in a corner.

We got off at the sixth floor and walked a short distance down the corridor. Mrs Mori let us in. I hadn't seen this apartment before, although I knew it was one with two storeys. I was surprised to see two fabulous curved staircases leading up to a galleried area. How they had done that, God only knows. They must have taken out the ceiling – it looked like the kind of entrance you'd find in a stately home.

Sakura led me into a wood-panelled room to the right of the hall.

'Chichi's mm . . . Dad office,' she said. To the left of an ornate desk was a tartan-covered sofa and on it was a huge bundle of fur: one white cat and one golden cat curled up around each other. I rushed over and the two cats perked up. They had such funny squashed faces and Chu appeared to recognise me because he nuzzled my hand with his nose.

'Brownie one Miyu, mean mm . . . beautiful moon,' said Sakura.

'She has a face like a moon,' I said as Miyu turned on her back and wriggled. I tickled her tummy and she purred loudly. *Sometimes I much prefer animals to people*, I thought as I remembered the scene upstairs. *These beasts have nothing to prove and love unconditionally*.

'You like drink something?' asked Sakura.

I got up and shook my head. 'No, my friends will be waiting for me, but thanks so much for letting me meet the cats.'

'You come anytime,' said Sakura. 'Can see you like and they like too.'

'I do,' I said. 'I like very much.'

Back on the fifth floor, the party was now in full swing. Cursed were playing up on the stage and people were dancing. I looked around for Pia. She was on the dance floor with Henry, while Charlie was doing the High-land fling with a pretty blonde girl. He'd taken off his wellies and she was wearing them. *Hmm, looks like he's scored there*, I thought. As soon as Pia and Henry noticed the Scottish dancing they joined in, flinging themselves around like maniacs. Alisha was also up dancing but in a group of people on the other side of the room. She didn't look happy. I didn't feel like danc-ing, so I edged myself into a corner in the hope that no-one would notice me.

'Hey, Jess,' said a male voice to my right. 'Awesome costume earlier.'

I turned to see JJ. He was looking very handsome in a black suit and the requisite *subtle* devil's horns.

'Oh! You knew it was me, then?' I asked, as Pia saw that I'd returned, waved and came over. Thankfully, she'd taken out the plastic zombie eyes.

'Oh yes. I knew it was you,' JJ replied. 'Hey, where did you get the wetsuit and flippers?'

'My swimming club,' I said. 'But I wish I hadn't. Not only did I look like a prat, I was boiling!'

'You looked cool . . . funny. And at least you didn't look like the rest of them,' he said as he indicated the room with a sweep of his hands.

'That's what Pia said, but you can see by her face that she is mentally deranged,' I said as, on cue, Pia made her eyes cross.

JJ laughed. 'So, do you swim, Jess?'

'She was our school champion last year,' said Pia. 'Jess doesn't just swim. She's like a fish in the water. She's up for the national school competition next month doing the crawl. She practises every day.'

JJ raised an eyebrow. 'So you're good, huh? Where do you swim?'

'Local baths,' I said.

'There's a great pool here,' said JJ. 'Have you seen it?'

'She swam there until she was told she couldn't,' said Pia, who seemed to have taken over my voice. I pulled on her arm to try and get her to shut up, but she was making an even stranger face than the one before, like she was trying to tell me something.

'Why not?' asked JJ.

'Staff,' I said. 'It's um . . . residents only.'

JJ looked serious. 'Is that right?'

'Yes, that is right,' said Alisha, suddenly appearing alongside her brother. I realised then what Pia had been trying to tell me – that Alisha was right behind us. 'If all the staff swam in our pool, it would be *public*, wouldn't it?'

'Well, I don't swim there any more, so you don't need to worry,' I said.

I hated the way she made me feel, like I would contaminate the water or something. And I hated the way that she'd said 'public'.

'Having a good time?' JJ asked his sister, changing the subject.

Alisha looked like her face was going to crumble. 'Actually, no,' she said. 'This so wasn't what I wanted.'

Not what you wanted? I thought. A dress to die for, a chance to make an entrance like a fairy princess, a room full of glam celebs – the whole thing was totally A-list, including the drinks and canapés!

'What more could you possibly want?' I blurted out before I could stop myself.

Alisha gave me the filthiest look. 'Well, I don't expect *you* to understand,' she said.

'Hey, come on, Alisha—' JJ started, but Alisha stomped off and out of the party room.

JJ turned to me and Pia. 'I apologise for my sister. She's been in a total strop about this party right from the beginning.'

Pia linked her arm through mine. What Alisha had said had hurt. How could she expect *me* to understand? That was harsh. Just because I wasn't rich? Just because I wasn't one of the A-list?

'Is she always like that?' Pia asked.

JJ sighed. 'No. Not at all. She's a good kid. Least she was until we moved here. I'm not trying to defend her behaviour – actually, yes, I am. See, this move has been tough on her. When we lived in California, Dad was the one who travelled when he had a movie and Mom,

Alisha and I stayed home – I mean, yeah, we'd visit him on set when we could, but Mom wanted us to have a stable base at home for school and stuff.'

'So why the change?' asked Pia.

'Dad's going to be working on his new movie over here for the best part of a year. He wanted to set up a base here so we could all be together. You should have seen Alisha the day we left. She was trying to put a brave face on it for Mom and Dad but she was in pieces. She had to leave all her friends behind, and she had some good ones back home, a tight bunch who she'd grown up with. That's why she's found it so hard meeting you guys. You're such good mates. She can see that you have what she has lost and you remind her of what she misses most.'

'I thought she meant I wouldn't understand because I'm not . . .' I gestured round the room, 'one of the in-crowd.'

'Nah. Doubt it. Not that. Knowing Alisha, she meant she didn't expect you to understand because you have your friends close by. How would you know what it's like to be lonely, away from the people you love?'

Pia glanced at me.

'I think I understand more than she realises,' I said.

Maybe I'd got Alisha wrong, I thought. Had I misjudged her? I imagined she had it all but maybe, underneath, we were more alike than either of us realised.

18

Sleepover

'So you're not going to invite her?' asked Pia as she plastered paint onto her bedroom wall. The colour that she had chosen was fuchsia, most of which had gone all over her face and T-shirt.

Her house was similar in layout to ours but already it looked different with all the bright colours that Pia and her mum had chosen. Jade green in the bathroom, deep gold in the living room, lilac in her mum's room and this vivid pink in Pia's bedroom. She wants to go for an Indian theme, with bright red and orange cushions and purple curtains. I didn't think it would work but already I can see that it's going to look exotic and warm.

'No,' I said, as I sloshed on another dollop of paint. 'I thought about it, and then I remembered the way she was that day we went shopping. She was so mean about my mum, as well as acting like a spoilt princess, so no. It's my birthday. I get to choose my own VIPs this time and that's you, Flo, Meg, Tom, Josh, Henry and Charlie.'

'A boy each, then. Cool.'

'Let's have a game of spin the bottle, then I can spin it and get it to stop at Henry so you can snog him.'

Pia blushed the same colour as the paint. 'As long as you don't stop it at Josh. Bleurgh.'

'Meg likes him, so you don't need to worry.'

'She must be mental, but I suppose *someone's* got to like him. And Flo likes Charlie and you like Tom. Sounds like a party to me!'

'Exactly,' I said. 'So who needs an odd one out messing things up? Though Meg and Flo would love to meet her . . .'

'And will madam be having a theme for her birthday, à la Alisha's?'

I nodded. 'Maybe. How about a Spanish theme and we could do some dancing?'

'Cool,' said Pia. 'I shall come flamenco-ed up.'

'And best of all, Dad said that I can have the summerhouse at the bottom of the garden as a den. OK, so I'll have to share it with Charlie, but he says he's not too bothered as long as I let him hang out there for band practice occasionally when they're not rehearsing at one of his mates' houses. He prefers to play away from Porchester Park in case one of les residents complains about the noise.'

'I thought your dad had bagged it.'

'He had, but he says that it's a waste of a good space

because he'll never get to use it. He's going to move the sunloungers down into a storage room in the basement of the apartment block, so the posh shed is mine.'

'Party on, my leetle Spanish chum,' said Pia, and she did a quick burst of flamenco. 'Olé!'

The following weekend, Flo and Meg came over to help deck out the summerhouse and it was soon renamed the VIP lounge. Meg did a great sign to put on the door saying **VIPs ONLY**. I loved it. My own hospitality suite and *I* got to choose who was on the list.

On the day of the party, I went out with Charlie to get some nibbles – crisps and tacos and dips – and as we were walking back up the road to the apartment block, I saw Alisha and her mum getting out of their limo.

Alisha saw us, hesitated, said something to her mum, then walked towards us.

'Prepare for the Queen of Insultland,' I whispered as she approached.

'Er . . . Jess, can I talk to you for a moment?' Alisha asked.

Oh God, what have I done now? I wondered. *What rule have I broken this time?*

'OK,' I said.

Alisha glanced at Charlie. He took the bags from me. 'I'll take these, Jess. See you at home later, yeah?'

I nodded.

As he strode off, Alisha and I stood in silence for a few moments.

'Want to come up to the apartment for a smoothie?' she asked. 'The ones our housekeeper makes are awesome. Raspberry and Greek yoghurt and honey.'

I was taken aback. Had Alisha Lewis just asked me up to her home?

'I . . . me? Would it be allowed?'

'You came to my party, didn't you? Anyway, I can have who I like over to my house and I . . . I want to say something to you.'

What was going on? Was she going to get me alone and then lay into me about something? *Only one way to find out*, I thought.

'OK. Sure.'

I followed her over the forecourt, where Yoram opened the door for us.

'Afternoon, Miss Lewis,' he said with a nod. 'Jess.'

'Miss Hall to you,' I replied. He arched an eyebrow. He wasn't amused, but Alisha actually laughed. *Somehow I've slipped into a parallel universe*, I thought as we crossed Reception to join Mrs Lewis at the lift. I was feeling very puzzled because Alisha wasn't saying much and I didn't know what to say either. My mind was racing with all sorts of stupid ideas – nice day (it wasn't, it was freezing), like your sneakers (I didn't – they were too pristine white), how's your home-schooling going? (Like I cared.)

'OK if I show Jess my room, Mom?' Alisha asked.

'Sure, hon,' she replied, and she gave me a sweet smile.

We got into the lift and went up to the apartment where Alisha led me into a room on the upper floor. I didn't let on that I'd seen the apartment before, although it looked more lived in than the last time I'd been up, with fresh flowers in the hall and magazines strewn across the sofa.

Upstairs, Alisha's bedroom was a dream and I couldn't help but say, 'Wow.' It was decorated in shades of gold and looked feminine but not too girlie. By the window was a chaise longue covered in sand-coloured velvet, the same colour as the silk bedspread.

'Like it?' she asked as she flopped onto the bed.

'Fab. Classy,' I said, and crossed to the window. 'And you have a great view of the park from up here.' I turned back to her and noticed that she looked awkward.

Best get it over with, I thought. 'So, what did you want to say?'

Alisha took a deep breath and sat up. 'I . . . I wanted to say I'm sorry.'

'Sorry? What for?' I asked, although I could think of about a million things and it was going to take a lot more than saying sorry to get me to forgive her.

'I know what you must think of me,' she blurted, 'and you'd be right, I've behaved like a total brat since I arrived here. I wanted to apologise and to say that I'm not really like that.' She grinned. 'At least not *all* of the time. I particularly wanted to say sorry about your mum and what I said that day we went shopping. I feel real bad about it.'

'You weren't to know,' I said. I knew I sounded more forgiving than I felt.

'Even so. I've been so stressed about it. I'm sorry I just walked away that day. I tried writing a card but the right words . . . it was a hard one to get right.' She sighed. 'Seems I've done everything wrong since I got here. I've felt mad about everything and everyone, about how my life's turned out. I've been pissed with the whole world. I so don't want to be here and feel so mad that my folks made me come. I've definitely taken it out on Mom and I guess . . . I guess I took some of it out on you, too, which wasn't fair.'

I shrugged. 'I thought you hated me.'

'Hated you? No way, Jess. I've been so jealous, I can't tell you.'

'Jealous? Of *me*? Why?'

'You and Pia. I look at you and I can see what great

mates you are – what fun you have, like at my party, you were brilliant.'

I couldn't take it in. 'Brilliant? But you said we were embarrassing. I thought you didn't want us there.'

Alisha's expression turned sad. 'Only because every time I see you, I'm reminded of what I haven't got any more – friends. Like at the party, all those people. You know, Mom *paid* some of them to come. I mean, how embarrassing is that? I think you and Pia and your brother and that other guy . . .'

'Henry.'

'Henry. You were the only people I even vaguely knew.' I saw tears glisten in Alisha's eyes. 'I've no real friends here.' She took a deep breath. 'I knew some great girls back in California. I really wanted them to come to my party. I would have preferred it if Mom had spent the money on flying some of them over rather than inviting a whole crowd of people who only wanted to come because it was a freebie and because I'm Jefferson Lewis's daughter. And that dress! *So* not what I wanted to wear. So not me. That's what I meant. It's so embarrassing after those great outfits that you and Pia picked out for me, but my mom made me wear it. You must have thought I looked like a right Barbie.'

'You looked beautiful,' I said. 'Boy, we really *have* been misunderstanding each other! I thought you meant that Pia and me were embarrassing.'

212

Alisha suddenly smiled. 'Well, you were a bit, you looked pretty crazy – but I loved that. It's just what my crowd would have done back home. No, I meant, how embarrassing it was that there I was, all done up like a princess in a long dress, even if it *was* Oscar de la Renta, while you'd taken the theme and had fun with it.'

'And I thought when you said that the party was so not what you wanted that you were throwing a wobbly.'

'I guess I was, in a way. But I didn't want more. I wanted less. I'd have liked a good old-fashioned sleep-over with my besties, like we used to have – to be with people I can be myself with, you know? I miss having someone to go down to the mall with, to hang out with and to watch a movie with in my PJs.'

'But it was such a great party,' I said.

'For everyone else,' said Alisha. 'Don't get me wrong. I love to party but it doesn't mean anything if you haven't got your friends with you. I felt so alone that night, surrounded by crowds. But I felt lonelier than ever when I saw you and Pia messing about. It only reminded me once again what a loser I am.' She looked so sad, like she was going to cry and, I couldn't help it, my heart went out to her.

I went over to sit next to her. I thought about putting my arm around her but hesitated. 'Hey, don't be sad. I know exactly how you feel. I do. When I first came to live here, I thought it was going to be so brilliant – you know, a fab apartment block, glam new people – but a few weeks in and I hated it. I missed my mates too. It was a huge readjustment, I can tell you.'

Alisha looked up. 'And you had that on top of your mum passing.'

Now I felt like *I* was going to cry.

'You must miss her,' said Alisha.

'Every single day.'

Alisha reached out, took my hand and squeezed it. 'I'm sorry you lost her.'

At that moment, I spotted a framed photo of a brown Labrador. 'Hey, who's that?' I asked, changing the subject.

Alisha glanced over to where I was looking. She got up and fetched the photo. 'Caspar.'

'Your dog?'

She nodded. 'I had to leave him behind too. Broke my heart, I can tell you. The look he gave me the day we left. I cried all the way to the airport. I've had him since he was a pup.'

'So why didn't you bring him? Residents can have pets.'

Alisha gestured around. 'A dog in a place like this?' She shook her head. 'I wouldn't do it to him. A dog needs space, outside access. He's used to acres of land. We left him with our housekeeper over there so I know he'll have a better life than he would here and I'll see him when I go back but, some days, I miss him so much it hurts.'

I got my wallet out and showed her the photo of Dave. 'Your cat?'

I nodded.

'He's adorable. Does he live with you downstairs?'

I shook my head. 'Staff aren't allowed to have pets.'

'That sucks.'

I nodded. 'He's with my gran. Broke my heart too,' I said, then I told her the whole story about hiding him in the summerhouse and him going and pooing on Dad's bed. She cracked up laughing. I watched her for a while.

'Hey, you know what, Alisha?'

'What?'

'You're OK and I guess I'm sorry too. I really thought you had it all.'

Alisha smiled wistfully. 'We've got a lot, don't get me wrong, but I miss Caspar and I miss my mates. I really *really* do.'

I glanced at my watch and stood up. 'Listen, I've got to go. I'm having a few mates over later so I have to get ready.'

'Sure,' said Alisha. I could see that she was trying to put on a brave face. 'It's been nice. So, what are you going to do? Watch TV? A movie?'

'It's my birthday and we're having a sleepover.'

'Cool. Of course. Sagittarian. I should have remembered. Happy Birthday,' Alisha said. She looked at the floor, but she couldn't hide how sad she was.

'Want to come?' I asked.

19

VIPs Only

Dad had a serious look on his face when he came through the front door. 'Er, Jess,' he said. 'I have another request from the Lewis household.'

'It's OK, Alisha and I are cool with each other now.' *At least I think we are.* Dad's expression said otherwise. Suddenly he broke into a huge grin.

'Not Alisha. JJ. Did you know he was on his school's swimming team back in California?'

I shook my head.

'Well, he was, and apparently he's been feeling that he's let his standard slip since he's been here.'

'So?'

'So, he's asked if you'd be willing to pace him.'

'Me? Pace him? Where? I don't think he'd like the local baths very much after what he's been used to.'

'He's asked if you'll swim with him here.'

'In the spa? But Mr Knight said I couldn't. Daughter of staff, blah blah.'

'A resident's request,' Dad beamed. 'How could he refuse? What do you say?'

A chance to spend time with JJ? A choice between swimming in the spa pool or the local baths with their musty changing rooms and kids getting in my way. Der? No contest, I thought.

'I'd rather have flesh-eating ants crawl over my face,' I said, and Dad's face fell. 'Joking. What time do I start?'

The rest of the afternoon was spent in a mad rush getting my VIP summerhouse ready. Henry and Charlie had already been in and pinned up an Indian bedspread that Gran had donated along with some scatter cushions and an old heater that she had stored up in her loft. Already it was warm, colourful and cosy.

At seven o'clock, Meg and Flo arrived bearing gifts and chocolates which we scoffed as we got ready. Pia had insisted I stay with the Spanish theme and had brought red frilly flamenco knickers for all of us. She and Flo immediately put them on their heads and I put mine over my jeans while Meg treated us all to a quick spurt of Spanish dancing.

Charlie popped his head round the door and rolled his eyes when he saw us. 'Girls are bonkers,' he said, and shut the door.

'You can talk,' I called after him.

Two minutes later, Charlie was back. 'You have a

guest,' he said and moved out of the way. Behind him stood Alisha, looking shyly in on us.

'Hi,' I said. 'Welcome to the madhouse.'

She looked very pretty in jeans and a blue top and held out a package for me. 'Happy Birthday, Jess,' she said.

I took the parcel, introduced everyone and they all insisted that I open my present there and then. Inside was the silver top we'd seen the day we'd gone shopping with her and her mum.

'Ohmigod!'

'I know you liked it,' she said. 'It's to say thanks for your help that day and also . . .' She looked at the others and didn't continue. I knew that she meant she was sorry for demanding to see my mum on the day we went shopping.

'Wow. Are you sure?' I said.

She nodded.

'I totally love it,' I said, and threw off my T-shirt, put the top on, and did a twirl while everyone ooh-ed and aah-ed. 'Thanks so much, Alisha.'

Pia stepped forward and handed Alisha a pair of fla-menco pants. 'It's a Spanish theme tonight,' she said. 'These are for you.'

'Thanks,' said Alisha and, seeing the way that Pia and Flo were wearing theirs, she immediately put her pair on her head.

Pants on the head, always an ice breaker, I thought. She was going to fit in just fine. I had invited JJ too but he was going out with his dad somewhere. I didn't mind that he couldn't make it because already we had a date to swim together one evening the following week, plus I wasn't sure how I'd feel having JJ and Tom in the same room. Confused.com, that would be me. Two gorgeous boys, but I wasn't sure I had a chance with either of them.

Five minutes later, Josh, Henry and Tom arrived and they all had a great laugh over the pants on head look. Josh was totally star-struck when he saw Alisha and for once was lost for words, which was a relief. Tom had brought a guitar with him and zoomed in on Charlie to talk music. He didn't seem at all fazed by Alisha being there, in fact, he appeared more into Chaz, acting like they were the best of old friends.

The rest of the evening passed in a haze of pizza, dancing, chatting and laughing. Everyone wanted to know about Alisha's life and she told us how much she missed her friends back home and how much of a readjustment the move to London had been.

'Dad wasn't always famous,' she said. 'We used to have a normal life until I was ten and Dad had his big hit, the movie *Star Eraser Five*. That changed everything.'

'I loved that film,' said Flo. 'Your dad was brill in it.'

'I'll tell him,' said Alisha.

'So how's it different now?' asked Pia.

'Dad's a public figure. Everyone wants a piece of him. They see him in a movie and think they know him, and us, like there are always journalists following us around wanting a story or a photo they can print, so we're not as free as we were. It's a different lifestyle totally. I'm not saying it's not fun. Of course, sometimes it is – most of the time – but you pay a price. Like, I never know if people want to know me just because I'm Jefferson Lewis's daughter, or not.'

'I have the same problem,' I said, with a glance at Tom who had hardly said a word to me all evening. 'Being related to Charlie, I never know whether people want to get to know me or him.'

Charlie rolled his eyes and Tom looked amused.

'It's true,' I said.

'Understandable,' said Alisha, and she gave Charlie a coy look. He blushed furiously. *Hmm. Interesting*, I thought, as Pia gave me a look to say that she'd clocked it too, though Flo didn't seem too happy.

'And Charlie is a fantastic musician,' said Tom.

'In that case,' said Pia, 'seeing as we have so much talent in the room, let's do an X *Factor* type game for a laugh. Everyone has to do an act and the rest of us will be the judges.'

'Nooo,' groaned Meg. 'I'm rubbish at everything.'

'All the better,' said Pia. 'The rubbish acts are always the most entertaining. Sorry Meg, there's no getting out of it, I'm afraid. Flo, you go first.'

Flo got up and fixed her eyes on Charlie. 'Some romantic music, maestro,' she said and Charlie began to strum a slow tune on his guitar. Flo began to dance a floaty, hippy type of dance with a lot of eye contact with Charlie. I couldn't help it, I got the giggles, and then so did Pia, Meg and Alisha. Flo didn't seem to notice, she was too busy waving her arms around and wiggling her bum for Charlie, who suddenly found the floor in front of him very interesting and refused to look up. I glanced at Tom and saw that he was watching me. This time, it was me who blushed furiously.

We clapped when Flo finished and everyone declared her brilliant – except for Charlie, who appeared to be having a coughing fit.

'You next, Meg,' said Pia.

Meg got up and did a tai chi display. She'd been doing classes on Saturday mornings. She was very good too, moving slowly and gracefully. Josh fell on the floor in front of her. 'Take me now,' he said. 'I'll be your slave for ever and worship at your feet.'

'In your dreams,' said Meg, but I could tell that she was secretly chuffed, until Josh made a dive for her calves and wrestled her to the floor. That boy never does know where to draw the line. *I must tell Charlie to give him some lessons in how to act with girls*, I thought, *or else Josh is destined to go through life single and wondering why*. Meg, however, is well schooled in all the martial arts and a swift karate chop to Josh's neck soon showed him who was in charge. He didn't seem to mind. *Maybe bashing each other about is their way of saying that they like each other*, I thought as I watched them wrestle on the floor.

Pia and I did a Highland fling and everyone joined in, even Tom, who dropped his cool act for a few minutes.

'Your turn, Alisha,' I said, when we'd stopped and caught our breath.

She shook her head. 'I can't do anything,' she said. 'Honest. No talent. Hands up, I admit it. When I was little, Beyoncé used to babysit us and she tried to teach me to sing and dance but still no luck. Tone deaf, flat feet, that's me.'

'You must be able to do *something*,' said Flo. 'Dance or sing or say a poem.'

'OK,' she said. 'I can do the splits.'

She slid down to the floor in the perfect position. 'Tadah!' she said.

Everyone clapped. 'Excellent, my dear,' I said. 'You can go through to the next round.'

Alisha got up from the floor, smiled and bowed.

'Josh, your go,' I said.

Josh got up. 'I am going to recite a poem,' he said. 'A very moving and deep poem.' He composed himself for a moment. 'Tarzan in the jungle, had a belly ache, couldn't find a toilet, th-wp, too late,' he said and stuck his bum out behind him. He bowed and sat down.

The rest of us looked at each other in amazement, then burst out laughing.

'Er, maybe you should think about another career rather than showbiz,' said Tom.

'No. Good try,' said Meg, and she looked coyly at Josh.

'Definitely different,' said Pia.

'No. I'm Simon Cowell and I say it was . . . rubbish! Possibly the worst act ever,' I said, and we all cracked up laughing again.

'I can light my farts,' said Josh. 'Anyone got a lighter?'

'There's a time to shut up, Josh, and that time is now,' I said.

'It *is* impressive,' he insisted.

'Josh, darling,' said Pia. 'If you are ever want to get anywhere in pulling girls, we can all assure you that lighting your farts is *not* a technique that has a lot of success.'

'Moving on,' I said. 'My party. No fart lighting. And that's final. Charlie, Tom,' I said. 'What are you going to do? See how far you can pee?'

Alisha cracked up laughing. 'My brother used to do that when he was a kid,' she said with a grin.

'How about we do the new number?' said Charlie and he nodded to Tom, who picked up his guitar.

'What key?' asked Tom.

'C,' Charlie replied.

'Er, excuse me,' I said. 'New number? C? Do you guys know each other?'

Charlie nodded. 'Yeah. I thought you knew. Tom called weeks ago and asked if we could meet up to play some music.'

All the pieces suddenly slotted into place. Tom asking for my number. Saying he wanted to spend more time with someone who lived at the apartment. It hadn't been *me* he'd wanted to call. It hadn't been one of the A-listers he'd wanted to get to know. It had been *Charlie*! They whispered together for a while and then took their places, Charlie on a stool, Tom standing behind him.

'OK. This is a new number I've written,' said Charlie, and he nodded to Tom. They began to play and Charlie sang:

'Hey, take a look at me, tell me what it is you see,
Chilled out perfection from my head to my toes
A stylish confection that everyone knows
Will soon grab two fistfuls of riches and fame

In life's needy lottery I'm on top of my game
Predestined, predicted, a winner from birth
But when I look in the mirror I just have to laugh
Coz the face looking back is wearing a mask
If only you could see through my eyes
To the real me behind this disguise . . .
Stream runs to the river, river flows to the sea,
Waves of emotion are washing through me
Adrift, lost and yearning to be who I am
But how will life treat me, just an honest man.'

As I listened and he went into the second verse, the words seemed to sum up so much of what I'd been feeling over the last few months. I felt a mixture of emotions – tenderness for Charlie for having said it all so well, and sadness at realising the turmoil he had clearly been going through too.

'Awesome,' I said, when they'd finished. 'I think you get to go through to the final.'

'You definitely have the X Factor,' said Flo as she looked straight at Charlie.

'Is there a prize?' asked Tom.

'You get to snog Jess,' blurted Pia. I could have killed her and went bright red. I glanced at Tom. He raised an eyebrow.

'Sounds good to me,' he said, and held my eyes for a few moments.

I felt my stomach do a back flip, front flip and nose dive into my toes and then back up to my head. 'Er . . . more supplies,' I blustered. 'Coke. Drink. I'll go and get . . . stuff.' I got up and fumbled for the door while Tom watched me with an amused twinkle in his eye. *Cool, cool, I must be cool*, I thought, but Meg stuck her foot out as I went by and I tripped straight over it and stumbled into Tom, who caught me.

'Oops,' I said, and scrambled to get my balance, but he pulled me back and put his arms around my waist

'So, my prize,' he said, and gave me a quizzical look.

'I, er—' I didn't manage to finish what I was about to say because he leant forward and kissed me softly on the lips. I felt myself melt and closed my eyes and kissed him back. It felt really really good.

'Hubba dubba,' said Pia.

'Oh, get a room,' said Meg.

'Er . . . does Charlie get a prize?' asked Flo, with a glance at Charlie.

'Er, I'm cool, thanks. Need a hand getting stuff, Jess?' he asked.

'No, fine, thanks,' I said. I felt myself blushing bright red as I attempted again to pull away from Tom, and this time, he let me go. As I got to the door, I turned back to him.

'You deffo go through to the next round,' I said, in

what was meant to be a deep, sultry voice but which came out as a squeak.

'Wahey,' cried Josh and dived on Meg, who was sitting on a beanbag. She tried to bash him off but he wasn't giving in. 'I want a prize too,' he insisted.

I left them wrestling and, with the torch that Gran had given me to guide me, I went inside to get more drinks and tacos. Chu was waiting on the patio. He meowed when he saw me.

'Naughty boy,' I said as I picked him up. 'You've escaped again!'

I carried him into the house, where Dad was watching TV. He immediately called Mr Mori, then gathered Chu up and set off to take him back. Shame, because I'd have liked to have taken him to the summerhouse to show my mates.

We'd just settled down to a game of spin the bottle (Flo's idea, she wasn't going to let Charlie off lightly), when Dad tapped on the summerhouse door. 'Mr Mori wants a word,' he said and beckoned me out to go back to the house with him.

I followed him across the garden and into the kitchen, where Mr Mori was waiting with Chu. He nodded when he saw me and I nodded back.

'Thank you, Jess,' he said. 'Sakura's very grateful. Chu seems to like you very much and Sakura asked me to ask something, a big favour of you and your father.'

Dad glanced at me.

'I'll do whatever I can to help,' I said, and Dad smiled.

'Because of my work, my family has to travel a few days just before New Year and then when our other daughter, Riko, has returned to school in January, we will be away again. Sakura always travels with us but she worries about her cats. They don't like being moved so . . . no obligation but she – we – wondered if we could ask you to look after them while we are away? They like you. Sakura likes you and feels they would be happier if they're allowed to settle in one place. And we'll pay, of course.'

I looked at Dad and he looked back at me as if to say, *What do you think?* A mad thought flashed through my head. *Go for it*, said a voice inside me. 'I would love to look after your cats but . . . er . . . instead of paying me, I wonder if . . .' I glanced at Dad. Would he be cross? *Nothing ventured, nothing gained*, I thought. I saw my rucksack in the corner of the room and raced over and pulled out my wallet. I showed Mr Mori the photo of Dave. 'This is my cat, Dave. He came with me when I moved but I had to send him back to my gran's because staff aren't allowed to keep pets. I miss him so much.' I glanced at Dad who was looking more and more worried by the minute. 'Like Sakura and her cats, I worry about Dave, so I have a big favour of my own to ask.

How about, instead of paying me, you sort of adopt Dave?'

Now it was Mr Mori's turn to look worried and he glanced over at Dad. 'You don't have to have him in your flat,' I continued, 'I'll keep him here and he will still be mine, but Mr Knight would *think* he was yours so he couldn't object.'

Dad looked shell-shocked. *Ohmigod, I've totally blown it*, I thought. *This time I've gone too far.*

'You keep Dave here but we adopt him to keep Mr Knight happy?' asked Mr Mori.

I nodded. Suddenly Mr Mori smiled and turned to Dad. 'Your daughter, she make a very good business lady. Do a good deal.'

'G . . . good deal?' Dad stuttered.

'Yes, and I do understand, Jess,' said Mr Mori. 'I understand how you girls like your pets. I like them too.'

Dad's shoulders dropped from where they were around his ears and he sighed with relief.

'I'll ask Sakura,' Mr Mori continued, 'but I know she'll say yes. She'd have twenty cats if I let her – but if this means her cats get looked after by you, who clearly love animals, we're all very happy, cats included. Good deal done.' He reached out to shake my hand.

I felt my heart soar as I shook his hand back, then

Dad saw Mr Mori and Chu to the front door. I turned to go back to my sleepover. *Dave can come back to me, Pia lives a stone's throw away and there's a very interesting game waiting to be played in the summerhouse,* I thought, as I skipped across the garden. *Result.*

20

Practise, Practise

'OK, Jess, let's go,' JJ called from the poolside on Thursday evening.

I took a last look at myself in the mirror in the changing room. I felt nervous about going out in front of him in my costume. What would he think of me? He probably used to hang out with perfect model type girls back in the States and might think I was a pale, skinny-looking weed. I turned to look at my side profile and sucked my stomach in. *Anyway, he's not interested in you as a girl*, I told myself, *he's interested in you as a swimming partner. And what about Tom?*

Although Tom hadn't asked me out on an official date, we'd had a few more snog sessions. At the sleep-over when we played spin the bottle and it was his turn, he'd deliberately stopped it at me then dived on me. It was fab. Mucho passionate. And again, on Tuesday after school, when he was round visiting Charlie and he saw me on the landing. He didn't say much, just pushed me against the wall, and kissed me hard. 'My motto when it comes to snogging is practise, practise,' he said with a cheeky grin, then went into Chaz's room leaving me wondering what he meant – did he think *I* needed to practise? Maybe he thought I wasn't very good at it, or was he just saying that *he* liked to practise? And this afternoon, when I was outside the library waiting to go in, he came up behind me and nuzzled into my neck. 'Zombie Queen,' he'd whispered. 'Having any more sleepovers?'

I didn't get a chance to reply because Mrs Callahan appeared at the end of the corridor and Tom leapt back before we got a telling-off.

I've tried asking Charlie if Tom ever mentions me to him, but if he does, Chaz isn't letting on. He says that they only talk about music when they get together.

'Come on, Jess,' JJ called again.

I made my way out and took a running jump into the water.

I swam over to where JJ was and took up my position.

'Crawl or breaststroke?'

'Crawl first,' I replied.

'OK, on your marks, get set, GO,' said JJ, and we were off.

We swam for about half an hour and I beat him twice. He beat me on the breaststroke and then we stopped to catch our breath.

'Not bad for a girl,' he said, with a grin.

'Cheek. I was going to say, not bad for a boy.'

'And hey, thanks for inviting Alisha the other night, she really enjoyed it.'

'We liked having her and I'm sorry you couldn't make it.' That was a lie. It might have been awkward with JJ there as well as Tom.

'Me too.' JJ's glance flickered down to my mouth, then back up to my eyes. I felt myself blush as I felt a pull of chemistry. *What's going on?* I asked myself. *Does he fancy me? And if he does, what do I do? Oh hell. Two gorgeous boys and maybe I* do *stand a chance with both of them.*

We swam for another half-hour and I really pushed myself to do my best – not only to prove I was as good as he was but also because the swimming championship would be happening in a few weeks and if I could keep up the practice with JJ, I would be in tip-top form.

'So,' said Pia, when she dropped into my house as I was having supper later the same evening. 'How's lover boy. Or is Tom lover boy?'

'Or is Henry?' I returned as I took a mouthful of macaroni cheese.

Pia sat down at the table opposite me. 'Don't try and avoid the question, Miss Hall. It's early days with Henry. I think he likes me but I'm not sure whether he *like* likes me, as in fancies me, or just thinks of me as a mate.'

'I think he *like* likes you. He was watching you a lot at the sleepover.'

'But he didn't make a move. Not like Tom.'

'Sometimes with boys, you have to let them know you like them first,' I said. 'I remember Mum saying that once. She said it's not easy for them in case they get turned down.'

'You never let on to Tom, though, did you?'

'Not really, apart from a few looks, but he's so confident. He's probably never been rejected.'

Pia nodded. 'Yeah. He knows he's a love god. Henry's cool and chilled with his mates but I don't think he's had many girls after him.'

'Maybe not, so there's no harm in you giving him a bit of encouragement. But Tom has lot of girls fancying him and it's early days with us, too. I don't know where I stand with him. Like, he said his motto about snogging is "practise, practise". Does he mean he wants to kiss lots of girls? Or just me? Or does he mean I need to practise? How do you know if you're a good snogger?'

Pia began to kiss the back of her hand. 'Practise, practise,' she said, then laughed.

'He's doing my head in, Pia, and we aren't even an official couple yet. I saw a love heart in the girl's loo at school with his name in it so I'm not the only one who fancies him.'

'Do you know who wrote it?'

'Nope.'

A few moments later, there was a ring at the door and Pia got up to answer it. It was Alisha and she came over and sat at the table.

'Hey,' she said. 'JJ said you'd be back from swimming. How did it go?'

'Umpf,' I said through a mouthful of food. 'He's good.'

'I hope you don't mind that I came over. It's so boring up at the flat.'

'Anytime,' I replied. I meant it too. I was looking forward to getting to know her better.

Pia sat at the other end of the table and glanced down at a sheet of paper that Dad had left there. She picked it up. 'It says confidential . . . I guess that means I shouldn't be reading it, huh?'

I nodded and snatched it away from her. 'Dead right,' I said, but I couldn't resist a quick peek at what was written on it. 'Hey, this is interesting. It's a list of new-bies who'll be on their way home for the holidays. Boys and girls coming home from school for Christmas: Alexei Petrov, aged sixteen; Riko Mori, aged fifteen. There's a whole page of them, some our age, some older.'

'Alexei Petrov?' said Pia. 'Isn't his dad a spy?'

'I don't know,' I replied. 'Is he?'

'Can't be a very good one if you know about it,' said Alisha.

'Either way, he sounds interesting,' said Pia, with a glance at her.

'Yeah. Cool,' said Alisha, and she grinned. 'Maybe a few boys for me to meet, now that you two are taken with Henry and Tom.'

Hmm, yeah. More boys. That's all I need! And it's not as if me or Pia are definitely going out with anyone. Maybe I should take Tom's advice and practise, practise. So either Tom, or JJ, or Alexei Petrov, whoever he is . . . he might be a contender. Whoever. Whatever. Life at Number 1, Porchester Park just got even more interesting!

21

The Last Race

'Are you ready, Jess?' asked Aunt Maddie.

'Yes. No. Yes,' I replied. Today was the day. It was my swimming race and I felt more nervous than ever, even though I'd spent the last few weeks practising, and pacing JJ in the spa. He hadn't made a move in the lurve department, but he was definitely flirty some days. I still wasn't sure how to react, in case he was one of those people who was just naturally charming and like that with everyone. I made a note to myself to try and watch him when a few more people were around and see how he was with them. My love affair with Tom hadn't developed beyond the occasional stolen kiss either and I was beginning to wonder if I was just one of a list of girlfriend wannabes. Boys. They do my head in.

The good thing was that Alisha often came down to watch JJ and me swim and afterwards we had drinks and snacks either at her place or at mine. I was so happy we were getting on so well. Beneath her tough act, she was fun, and I could see she'd be a loyal friend. We were actually alike in so many ways and into all the same TV programmes, movies and music. Dave had taken to her too – and he can be very sniffy when he first meets people, but they were great pals straightaway.

I was still over the moon about the new arrangement. Mr Knight couldn't object and didn't and the Moris agreed that although they had 'adopted' Dave, he was to stay with me in our house. When they were away, I'd go up and look after their cats in their apartment. Sorted. It wasn't going to be a big deal because they had a housekeeper there to feed them. My job was to go up and give them some love and attention. No problem. It was a job I was looking forward to.

'Let's go,' called Gran, from downstairs. She and Aunt Maddie were taking me to the pool as Dad was having to work, but he'd promised he'd be there in time for my race.

I threw my swimming things in a bag and looked in the mirror. I took a deep breath. 'Right. Let's do it,' I said to my reflection.

The event was being held at the local swimming pool. My race wasn't until later so I took a seat to watch in the benches alongside Aunt Maddie, Gran, Pia and Charlie. Eight schools had made it to the finals and we watched the first contenders nervously pacing the side of the pool, ready for the first event which was a synchronised swim. When they hit the water, it looked like mayhem as twenty-four swimmers sploshed about doing their loosening-up exercises. On the whistle, they took their places then struck out together, every stroke, kick and wave in harmony. With hardly a ripple, they formed a flower pattern and I watched with admiration as the petals opened and closed in perfect time with the music.

'When's your race?' asked Charlie.

'Last,' I said. 'They always have the girls' front crawl last.'

'You'll be fine,' said Charlie. 'You've put in the work and you're going to win.'

'I might do, but whether our school wins depends on the collective score,' I said. 'One of our best swimmers pulled a muscle so our chances in the third race aren't so strong.'

After the synchronised swimming, I watched as the lanes in the pool were sectioned off with bright red ropes and the competitors lined up for the breaststroke. That was my cue to go and get ready. Everyone in the changing rooms was hyped up and talking about who we were up against – it appeared that Red Lodge High and Raynes Hill were our main competitors.

'Stay calm, stay focused and above all, remember your breathing,' Mr Bennie said as we trooped out after him to take our places on the competitors' benches. The breaststroke final was over and the swimmers for the backstroke were already in the water. The whistle blew and they were off. I glanced up to look for my crowd of supporters and saw that Tom, Flo and Meg had arrived and, to my delight, sitting next to them were Alisha and JJ, with Sergei on the bench behind. *Ohmigod*, I thought as a flood of panic hit me. I was OK swimming in front of others on the team but performing in public was starting to do my head in. There was still no sign of Dad, though. I felt so disappointed that he hadn't shown yet. He knew how important it was to me. He'd been making such an effort to spend more time with Charlie and me lately and I so wished he was here.

I felt as if an icy hand had gripped my stomach. 'Sir, I need the bathroom,' I said. Mr Bennie gave me a nod and as I dashed to the loo, I tried to keep breathing correctly but found I could hardly breathe at all. I returned to the benches minutes later to hear an ear-splitting roar as Raynes Hill won the last race. I glanced at the scoreboard. Red Lodge were in the lead with twenty-four points, Raynes Hill second, our school, West Bailey High, a miserable third. The knot in my stomach grew even tighter.

Mr Bennie saw me looking at the results. 'We're all depending on you now, Jess.'

'No pressure, then,' I said.

'You can do it,' Mr Bennie said, with a confidence I wish I shared.

'Mmf,' I said. My legs felt like jelly, my stomach was churning and I felt like I was going to throw up at any moment. I had a feeling the display the audience was going to get was of the technicolour chunder variety. *I can't do it*, I thought. I put my hands up to my temples and pressed hard. *Shut up, shut up*, I told myself. *Relax, breathe – oh God, I need the loo again.*

I watched the rest of the races in a daze. Our team was holding its own and then, in the butterfly final, our captain, Hayley Johnson, surged ahead. The scoreboard showed that we were equal with Red Lodge with one hundred and thirty-five points. Suddenly it was time for my race. Mr Bennie called me forward.

'We can still do it, Jess. The record for the crawl is sixty-seven seconds. You've done it in sixty-four in practice. If you can win the race *and* beat the record, we'll get double score, ten points and we'll be top school. So, clear your mind, forget where you are and go for it.'

I wobbled to my feet. 'I can't even walk, never mind swim.'

'Positive thinking, Hall, positive thinking!' said Mr Bennie.

'What? Like sink or swim?'

Mr Bennie chuckled. 'Something like that.'

I did a weak thumbs up and took my place on the starting block. Last year, even though Mum had been unwell, she'd insisted on being there – as she had been for every swimming contest I'd ever entered. An image of her last appearance amongst the spectators flashed through my mind. She'd been wearing one of her mad caps – a yellow one with great blue plastic flowers stuck on the side of it. She'd made Charlie wear one too and he'd been so embarrassed. *For luck*, she'd said, and, *Never forget it's supposed to be fun*.

I stretched and steadied my breathing. I felt such a longing for Mum, for a hug from her to see me through. But she wasn't there – and nor was Dad. I'd just have to do it by myself.

I sneaked a last look at my group of family and friends to see if Dad had made it. I. Could. Not. Believe. It. Charlie was waving like mad and looking very pleased with himself. He, Pia, Meg and Flo were all wearing yellow bathing caps with blue flowers stuck on the side – even Tom, Alisha and JJ were wearing them! I quickly scanned the crowd for Dad and, double phew, there he was, pushing his way along the row, trying to find his seat before the race started. He saw me looking, grinned and waved. Charlie handed him a yellow cap too and I couldn't help but smile as Dad pulled it on to his head. I was so glad he'd made it. I knew he had to work hard, but he was trying to be a good dad too.

And suddenly I forgot about everyone else, the crowd watching, the number of points I had to achieve. *I'm going to swim for you, Mum,* I thought. *I'm going to make you proud.*

The whistle blew and I dived in. I imagined Mum at the end of the pool, as she had been so many times before when I was little and just learning. I remembered her urging me on, telling me I could do it as I sank and paddled, gasping for breath. In a flash, I realised she lived on in me, she would always be there and nothing could ever take her memory away. I could feel her urging me on, not just in the race but in my whole life, her voice saying, 'You can do it, Jess. You *can.*'

My legs had never felt more powerful, my arms tore through the water, stroke after stroke after stroke. At the turn, I saw a flash of a red costume in the lane next to me and knew it was just me and a girl from Red Lodge. 'You can do it,' urged Mum's voice in my head. Seconds later, I touched the pool edge and it was all over. I pulled myself out of the water to see the girl from Red Lodge still a fraction behind me. I heard a cheer that almost lifted the roof and, seconds later, I was being mobbed by my team-mates.

'You did it, Jess!' said Hayley. 'You did it! Sixty-three seconds!'

I'd beaten the inter-school record *and* my own. I glanced up at the board to see the electronic numbers flicker and change.

West Bailey High: 145 points.

Red Lodge High: 139 points.

We'd won.

Our team dashed back to the changing rooms to grab our robes and then back out for the prize-giving.

A fanfare of trumpets burst out from the PA and a man's voice said, 'Ladies and gentlemen, it gives me great pleasure to announce the final result in the Inter-school Swimming Challenge Shield. After an exceptional competition day, in third place, we have Raynes Hill.' There were cheers from the crowd as their swimming team went forward to receive their medals. After them, second place was announced to Red Lodge High.

And then it was our turn and, to deafening applause and the stamping of feet, we made our way to the podium at the top of the baths to receive the shield. Mr Bennie stepped forward to take it from the mayor, then handed it to me. I waved it at the crowd and then handed it to Hayley. I knew she'd done her best, too. She held it aloft and the crowd cheered again.

The judges then moved on to the special commendations.

Barry Humphrey for the backstroke.

Steve Thomas for the butterfly stroke.

Jane Kennedy for breaststroke.

'And now our crawl champion for the second year running, Jessica Hall,' said the mayor and he beckoned me forward. I took a deep breath, stepped forward and took my medal and sash from him, then glanced up at my crowd. I burst out laughing. They were still wearing the swimming caps and jumping up and down like idiots. I felt a lump come to my throat. Mum wasn't there this time but Dad was, and maybe, just maybe, she was looking down on us all from somewhere. If she was, I knew that she'd be wearing a mad cap too. Maybe one with wings on, instead of flowers.

As the crowd began to disperse and the swimmers made their way back to the changing rooms, Alisha and JJ suddenly appeared at the poolside, waving frantically.

'Jess, over here. We have something for you,' JJ called, as they were joined by Pia, Meg, Flo, Charlie and Tom.

I turned back and went over to them.

Alisha handed her bag to JJ. 'I think you should do the honours, bro,' she said.

'Love to,' said JJ, and he pulled a sparkling tiara out of Alisha's bag. He stepped forward, made a low bow then put the crown on my head.

'I now pronounce you . . . er, what shall we call you? I know – barefoot princess,' he said, then leant forward, kissed my cheek and gave me a hug. 'Congratulations, swimming pardner.'

Behind him, Meg, Flo, Pia and Charlie curtseyed, and Pia raised an eyebrow at me, which I ignored. I noticed that Tom didn't curtsey. He was looking at JJ with a quizzical expression. *I'm not going to worry about this now*, I decided. It was too good a moment to ruin and it wasn't as if anything had exactly happened between myself and JJ, at least nothing for Tom to be jealous of. It wasn't as if he and I were even a real couple. Boys. Who knew what they were about? All I knew was that today wasn't the day to worry about it. If either of them were serious, no doubt it would become clear in the future. In the meantime, I was going to enjoy the attention. I'd just been crowned a princess!

'Liked the bathing caps, Chaz,' I said.

'Mum would have expected it,' he said. 'She'd have been so proud of you, Jess.' I knew he understood exactly.

It doesn't get any better than this, I thought as I looked at all my mates standing there.

'Thank you,' I said. 'For being here and for looking like such complete idiots. You're mates in a million.'

Pia grinned and pointed at Alisha and JJ. 'They really are,' she said. 'Million dollar mates.'

I shrugged and linked arms with her and Alisha. 'Same thing to me. Mates. That's the bit that counts.'

**If you enjoyed *Million Dollar Mates,*
look out for the sequel, *Paparazzi Princess,*
coming soon!**

It's the end of term and Jess is excited about all the new faces due to arrive at Number 1, Porchester Park for the holidays. Outside the apartment block, the usual paparazzi lie in wait hoping for a story or photo. Jess knows she should avoid them, and when new resident Riko arrives, they enjoy dodging the cameras together. But is Riko all she appears to be – or is this million dollar mate a fake?

Distracted by two boys: handsome A-lister JJ and school babe magnet Tom – neither of whom are making their intentions totally clear – Jess is finding it really hard to know who to trust right now.

And getting it wrong could prove to be a costly mistake . . .

About the Author

Cathy Hopkins lives in Bath, England with her husband and three cats, Dixie, Georgia and Otis. Cathy has been writing since 1986 and started writing teenage fiction in 2000. She spends most of her time in her writing turret pretending to write books but is actually in there listening to music, hippie dancing and checking her facebook page. So far Cathy has had fifty three books published, some of which are available in thirty three languages.

She is looking for the answers to why we're here, where we've come from and what it's all about. She is also looking for the perfect hairdresser. Apart from that, Cathy has joined the gym and spends more time than is good for her making up excuses as to why she hasn't got time to go. You can visit her on Facebook, or at www.cathyhopkins.com